A SPECIAL FRIENDSHIP

"You like Gabriella as a friend?" Nikki asked cautiously.

"Yeah. Why? Don't you like Carrie?"

Nikki studied Haley for a minute before answering. She watched as Haley tied her hair up in a ponytail.

"I guess I don't know Carrie," she admitted. "I don't know if I like her or not. Look, Haley—that's what I wanted to talk to you about. The truth is that I've never actually met a—a—" Nikki searched for the right word.

"A person with Down syndrome?" Haley asked.

"A person who's retarded in any way," Nikki admitted.

"Ever?" Haley's eyes were wide with surprise.

"Ever," said Nikki.

THE WINNING SPIRIT

Melissa Lowell

Created by Parachute Press

A SKYLARK BOOK
NEW YORK · TORONTO · LONDON · SYDNEY · AUCKLAND

RL 5, IL ages 9–12

THE WINNING SPIRIT
A Skylark Book / October 1995

Skylark Books is a registered trademark of Bantam Books, a division of Bantam Doubleday Dell Publishing Group, Inc. Registered in the U.S. Patent and Trademark Office and elsewhere.

Unified Sports® is a registered trademark of Special Olympics International.

Series design: Barbara Berger

ISBN 0-553-48321-8

Published simultaneously in the United States and Canada

Bantam Books are published by Bantam Books, a division of Bantam Doubleday Dell Publishing Group, Inc. Its trademark, consisting of the words "Bantam Books" and the portrayal of a rooster, is Registered in the U.S. Patent and Trademark Office and in other countries. Marca Registrada. Bantam Books, 1540 Broadway, New York, New York 10036.

PRINTED IN THE UNITED STATES OF AMERICA

OPM 0 9 8 7 6 5 4 3 2 1

1

Nikki Simon's green eyes sparkled as she sat on a bench braiding her long brown hair. Behind her, she could hear the Zamboni smoothing down the ice of the Seneca Hills Ice Arena.

It was a Monday afternoon in early October. As she did every afternoon except Sunday, Nikki had been practicing at the ice rink. She belonged to a skating club called Silver Blades. And that day she had just had one of the best practice sessions ever. She and her pairs partner, Alex Beekman, had performed the difficult triple loop–Lutz combo. Nikki still felt as if she were soaring through the air.

"You're Nikki Simon, aren't you?" The voice startled her.

Nikki looked up from her braid and smiled. "Yes. That's me."

A small, delicate-looking Hispanic girl stood before Nikki. She had dark hair and black almond-shaped eyes.

"I've seen you skate," said the girl. "You're fantastic!"

Nikki's smile widened, revealing a row of silver braces along her upper teeth. "Are you a skater?" she asked politely.

"I am. I love to skate." The girl stared adoringly at Nikki.

Nikki wasn't quite sure what to say. "So, how often do you skate?" she asked.

"Every day," the girl responded.

Nikki frowned. She knew that couldn't be true. Only the members of Silver Blades skated at the arena every day. Nikki examined the girl more closely.

"Do you mind if I ask how old you are?"

"I'm nine," the girl said simply.

Nikki would have guessed seven. The girl was small. But it wasn't only the way she looked that made her seem young. It was also the way she spoke: sort of slow and deliberate.

"Do you *really* skate here every day?" Nikki asked.

"I really do skate every day," the girl announced proudly. "But I hardly ever skate here."

Nikki suddenly felt embarrassed. Why had she assumed the girl was lying?

At that moment, Haley Arthur leaped onto the bench next to Nikki. Haley was another pairs skater in Silver Blades. And she was one of Nikki's best friends.

"What a triple loop–Lutz combo you and Alex did!" Haley said.

"It *was* pretty great, wasn't it?" Nikki admitted.

"Great? It was amazing," Haley exclaimed as she stuffed her hair up into a baseball cap. Haley was a total tomboy. That day she was wearing baggy jeans with black combat boots.

"Hi, Gabriella!" Haley said to the younger girl.

"Hi, Haley." Gabriella gave her a wide smile.

"How's the Olympic training going?" Haley asked.

The Olympics? thought Nikki. A nine-year-old training for the Olympics?

Skaters like Nikki worked their whole lives hoping that one day, if they were talented and lucky, they would qualify for the Olympics. How could a nine-year-old have already made the team? And how did Haley know her, anyway?

"You're training for the Olympics?" Nikki asked Gabriella. Gabriella nodded.

"So—how *is* it going?" Haley repeated.

"Not so good," replied Gabriella sadly.

"Why not?" asked Haley.

"Well, they kind of canceled skating camp," she explained.

"Oh, no. Why?" Haley cried.

"I'm not sure." Gabriella shrugged. "We heard two different things. No place to practice. Not enough coaches. And I know what that means. No practice, no Olympics."

Nikki watched Haley as Gabriella spoke. She wondered if Haley also thought that there was something a little off about Gabriella. It seemed as if speaking was an effort for her.

But Haley didn't seem to notice. She was completely focused on what Gabriella was saying.

"That stinks!" said Haley.

"Yeah," Gabriella said, sounding dejected.

For a moment Nikki thought Gabriella was going to burst into tears. But instead she pulled her small frame up straight. "Have you seen Martina?" she asked, naming another Silver Blades skater.

"Um, yeah—I think she's in the locker room." Haley pointed at the room behind them.

"Thanks." Gabriella smiled shyly at Nikki. "Nice meeting you," she said.

"You too," Nikki answered. She watched Gabriella as the younger girl headed toward the locker room.

Nikki's mind was racing again. She turned to Haley. "Is Gabriella a friend of Martina's?" she asked.

Haley grinned and rolled her eyes. "She's Martina's sister, silly!"

"She is?" Nikki exclaimed, surprised.

"Sure," Haley teased. "Isn't Martina allowed to have a sister?"

Nikki shifted uncomfortably in her seat. "It's not that. It's just that you said it like I should have known."

"Well, don't you think they look alike?" asked Haley.

"Not all sisters look alike," Nikki replied, defending herself. Although now that she thought about it, Martina and Gabriella looked *a lot* alike. Except for the eyes.

Martina Nemo had joined Silver Blades more than a year before, even before Nikki had become a member. But they had never become friends. They had different skating coaches, and Martina was in the ninth grade, a year ahead of Nikki. So Nikki didn't know much about Martina or her family.

"Have you ever seen Gabriella skate?" Nikki asked Haley. "Is she good?"

"Really good," Haley answered. "I skated with her a few weekends ago during free skate. We skated pairs. It was a lot of fun. She's much better than I thought she would be."

"Really?" said Nikki. "Good enough to be in the Olympics?"

Haley nodded. "Sure. Why not?"

Nikki shrugged. There was just something different—something a little strange—about Gabriella. But she didn't want to say that to Haley.

"I don't know," she said instead. "She's kind of young, I guess."

"She may be young," said Haley, "but she's good. She's a cinch to win a medal at the Special Olympics figure-skating competition."

Special Olympics! That explained it. Special Olympics was a program for people with mental disabilities.

Nikki laughed. "Special Olympics! Now I get it."

"You thought it was the Olympic Games?" Haley said. "A nine-year-old?"

"That's why I was so confused," Nikki admitted.

Haley grinned at her. "Well, Gabriella's been competing in Special Olympics for a few years now."

"Wow," said Nikki, impressed. "I guess she really is good!"

Haley nodded. "She is. And the Special Olympics skating competition is really a great event. I went last year."

Nikki hesitated. "So—so what's wrong with her?" she finally asked.

"Nothing!" Gabriella chirped from behind Nikki.

Nikki thought she would die of embarrassment. She turned around. Gabriella was standing right behind her with her sister, Martina.

"I—I'm sorry," Nikki stammered.

"It's okay," Martina answered in a musical voice. With her olive-colored skin and big brown eyes, Martina *did* look a lot like Gabriella. "Lots of people don't know how to behave around Gaby," Martina said. "Right, squirt?" She nudged her sister.

"Don't call me squirt," Gabriella squealed.

"Sorry, pip-squeak," Martina said, grinning.

Gabriella dissolved into a fit of giggles and playfully punched Martina.

"The only thing wrong with Gabriella," Martina explained to Nikki, "is that she giggles too much."

Gabriella stopped giggling. "Don't say that, Tina," she said. She turned to Nikki. "I'm slower than a lot of people. But I can do lots of things everyone else does.

I go to a regular school. I ice-skate, and I do other stuff too. Okay?"

"Okay." Nikki felt uncomfortable and impressed at the same time.

"I really can skate pretty well, huh, Haley?" Gabriella asked.

"You sure can!" said Haley. "That was so much fun when we skated together. I wish we could skate pairs in Special Olympics."

"You mean there's no pairs skating in Special Olympics?" Nikki asked.

"There is!" Gabriella practically shouted. Nikki could see how excited the idea of pairs skating made the young skater. "There's a new event this year. I could skate with one of you," Gabriella added. She raised her arms and danced around the floor as if she were skating with a partner.

"Really?" Nikki asked. "One of us?"

"Yes!" Gabriella was suddenly serious. "Unified Similar Pairs," she said. "Two girls can skate together."

Nikki watched in amazement as Haley leaned forward, eagerly listening to what Gabriella was saying. It was as if she was actually considering skating pairs with a Special Olympics skater. Nikki couldn't believe it. Was Haley out of her mind?

Maybe Haley was just being nice. After all, Haley had no time to fool around with someone who wasn't a serious skater. Silver Blades skaters had their own competitions to worry about.

A woman appeared inside the entrance to the Ice Arena. Gabriella noticed her and gasped. "Mom!" she cried. "Oh, Tina, Mom's been waiting outside this whole time. I forgot!"

Martina waved at her mother, then turned to her friends. "We've got to go," she said.

Martina and Gabriella said their good-byes and raced outside. As Haley watched them leave she shook her head sadly.

"I can't believe they canceled Gabriella's skating camp. It really is too bad," Haley told Nikki.

Nikki shrugged. "Yeah, I guess so."

"You guess so? It's more like a disaster," Haley cried.

Nikki was taken aback. "Listen, I don't want to sound mean or anything, but it's not the end of the world."

"It is to Gabriella," said Haley. "And it would be to you."

"To me? It isn't the same thing," said Nikki.

"Sure it is," Haley insisted.

Nikki shook her head. Didn't Haley see the difference? "But it isn't the same, Haley. We live for ice-skating. We eat, breathe, and dream ice-skating."

"So does Gabriella," Haley said. "She loves to skate. She skates as often as she can. Just because she isn't in a club like Silver Blades doesn't mean that skating isn't as important to her as it is to us."

Nikki didn't answer. She couldn't believe what she was hearing. Nikki, Haley, and the other members of Silver Blades sacrificed everything for skating. Six days a week, they got up early to practice before school, and practiced again after school. Special Olympics was a nice idea, but it wasn't for serious athletes.

"I wish there was something I could do to help," Haley said.

"Like what?" Nikki asked.

"I don't know. Maybe I could meet Gabriella here on Sundays. Or maybe I could help coach her or something."

"What for?" Nikki frowned. "You're not going to compete with her."

Haley studied Nikki. "What if I did coach her? Would there be something wrong with that?"

"No, not at all." Nikki was feeling more misunderstood every time she opened her mouth. "I just meant that practicing one day a week isn't enough. If skating really means so much to Gabriella, that would only frustrate her more."

"Yeah, you're right," Haley agreed. "But maybe there's some way to coach her every day." She rested her chin in the palms of her hands. Nikki could see that she was deep in thought.

"Haley, why is this so important to you?" Nikki asked suddenly.

"I don't know," said Haley, staring at the floor. "I like Gabriella. And she really loves skating." She paused. "If the same thing was happening to Silver Blades, other people would want to help us."

Nikki gathered her belongings as she searched her

mind for something hopeful to say. "It's too bad they can't train here," she finally told Haley. She stood up to leave.

Haley leaped to her feet. "That's it!" she cried. She sprang to Nikki's side. "That's the perfect answer. We can take care of both of their problems—no place to practice and not enough coaches." Haley beamed at Nikki. "The Special Olympics skaters can train here. And *we* can be their coaches! I'm so excited, I've got to ask Mr. Weiler right now. Thanks so much, Nikki. You're a genius!"

Haley kissed Nikki and raced toward Mr. Weiler's office.

Frozen to the spot, Nikki watched her go. Her mind was swimming with confusion. What had she done?

2

Later that night Nikki was struggling with her homework when her mother called up the stairs. "Haley's on the phone!" she shouted.

Nikki ran out to the hallway and picked up the phone. "Hi! You saved me from math," she said into the receiver.

"Plus I have great news!" Haley said excitedly.

Nikki felt her stomach churn. She was afraid she already knew what the news would be. And she wasn't too crazy about it.

"What news?" she asked as cheerfully as she could.

"Mr. Weiler wasn't at the rink earlier, but I talked to Kathy," Haley answered. "And she thinks that having the Special Olympics skaters train with us is a fantastic idea!"

"She does?" Nikki tried to sound more enthusiastic than she felt.

"Yep!" said Haley. "She's going to talk to Mr. Weiler about it tonight. Isn't that great?"

"Yeah. Great."

"Well, gotta run," Haley said. "I've already told Tori and Martina. Now I want to call Jill and Patrick."

"What did Tori say?" Nikki asked.

"She loved the idea!" said Haley. "Who wouldn't? And we owe it all to you. Thanks again, Nik. See you tomorrow."

Nikki hung up the phone. She felt stunned. It really wasn't my idea, she wanted to shout. She had only been trying to make Haley feel better.

Well, I did do that, Nikki thought, smiling to herself. Haley was definitely feeling on top of the world. The problem was, Nikki wasn't. She was feeling . . . She couldn't quite put her finger on it. Maybe her mom could help.

Nikki found her mother in the nursery, sitting in a rocking chair and singing to Nikki's five-month-old baby brother.

"Hey, Benji!" Nikki cooed at the sleepy infant.

Benji gurgled back.

"Can I play with him, Mom?" Nikki asked.

"Well, I was hoping he would go to sleep," said Mrs. Simon.

"Oh, come on, Mom. He can sleep anytime," Nikki pleaded.

Mrs. Simon stifled a yawn, then smiled at her daughter. "Actually, he does sleep anytime," she said. "Just not through the night. And with your father working extra hours at the office, I'm on call twenty-four hours a day."

Nikki bent down, scooped her baby brother into her arms, and nuzzled his neck. She loved the way he smelled. Was it the baby powder her mother put on him that made him smell so wonderful? Her father once said that babies smelled good so their parents would put up with all their crying and diaper changing and spitting up. It works for sisters, too, Nikki thought, giving the infant a kiss.

"How was practice today?" Mrs. Simon asked, yawning again.

"It was great!" said Nikki. "Alex and I did a perfect triple loop–Lutz combo!"

"Really?" said Mrs. Simon eagerly. "Honey, that's wonderful. So that's why Haley sounded so excited on the phone."

"Actually, Haley is excited for a different reason." Nikki handed the squirming Benjamin back to her mother. "She wants some Special Olympics skaters to train at the Seneca Hills rink. Silver Blades members will be their coaches."

"Sounds like a rewarding challenge." Mrs. Simon bent over Benjamin as he started crying. "Honey, hand me the pacifier, please."

Nikki handed her mom the pacifier. "I don't think

you understand, Mom," she continued. "This will really cut into our practice time. And we're students, not teachers."

Mrs. Simon shrugged, holding Benjamin's pacifier in his mouth. "It could be a good experience for all of you," she said.

At that moment, Ben started screaming and rocking his head from side to side.

Nikki was frightened. "What's wrong with him?" she asked. "He's never done that before."

"I don't know, honey." Mrs. Simon put the baby over her shoulder and gently patted his back. "Nobody knows exactly what little babies fuss about."

"But something's wrong," Nikki said. "Isn't it?"

"No, Nik. He's probably either hungry or tired. Maybe he has gas or he's cranky or bored. In other words, he's totally normal. Now, why don't you go finish your homework, and we'll continue this conversation later?"

As nice as her mother was being, Nikki could tell that a screaming baby and a daughter asking questions at the same time was too much for her.

"Sure, Mom. Later." Nikki slipped out of the room. They didn't have to continue the conversation, though. There was nothing else to talk about. Kathy, Tori, and even Nikki's mother thought Haley's idea was great. Nikki would have to sleep on it. Maybe in the morning she would think it was a great idea, too.

But when she woke up, the idea still made Nikki uncomfortable. And it was getting in the way of her skating.

On Wednesday morning, before the scheduled Special Olympics meeting, Nikki's skating was particularly disastrous.

Out on the ice, Kathy Bart shook her head in disappointment. The coach's dark blond ponytail swung back and forth.

"Okay, you two. That's it for the day," the coach told Nikki and Alex. "Maybe afternoon practice will be better."

It was only six-thirty. Usually they practiced until seven.

"Can't we please try it one more time?" Nikki pleaded. "I didn't come out of the spin right."

"No, it was my fault," Alex said. Bending over from the waist, he put his hands on his thighs and tried to catch his breath. "I didn't set you up right."

"Actually, you were both at fault," Kathy said. "But there isn't time to try it again. The Special Olympics meeting starts in five minutes."

Alex threw a towel over his shoulders. "Coaching those kids is going to be fun. You really had a great idea, Nikki."

"Yeah. I guess." Nikki could add Alex to the list of people who thought her idea was terrific. When was Nikki going to start liking it more?

Nikki went to get changed. When she came out of the dressing room, she headed straight for the bleachers. The other members of Silver Blades were already there, talking and milling about. She quickly scanned the sea of light blue warm-up jackets for her friends. Jill Wong was sitting five rows up in the stands.

Jill was one of Nikki's closest friends, and the best skater in Silver Blades. Or she used to be the best— before she had injured her ankle. Now she spent most of her time in physical therapy. Strengthening her ankle was proving to be a slow process, but Jill worked at it with as much determination as ever. She had always worked hard at her skating. Nikki really admired Jill.

Sitting on one side of Jill was Tori Carsen, a pretty blonde, who was also a close friend of Nikki's. Nikki sat down beside them and smiled. Both girls smiled back.

"Where's Haley?" Nikki asked.

Tori shrugged. "I don't know," she said. "I can't believe she's late. She's so excited about this meeting."

Alex settled himself onto the seat next to Nikki. He had just started to ask Nikki about the spin they messed up when a deep voice boomed through the arena.

"Settle down!"

A hush quickly descended on the room. Franz Weiler stepped before the bleachers. The head coach of Silver Blades was both loved and feared by his students. They knew that he had been one of the best skaters around in his day. He had since coached many skaters to Olympic medals.

"So, you think you can be coaches?" he said. "You think that coaching is easy, hmmm?"

Laughter rippled through the bleachers. Nikki scanned the group for Haley, but could find no sign of her friend.

Mr. Weiler continued. "Kathy and I have spent a lot of time discussing the idea of working with the Special Olympics skaters," he said, then paused for a moment. "We have decided that it is an excellent plan! We will begin immediately."

Some members of Silver Blades started clapping and cheering. Others were talking loudly among themselves. Mr. Weiler held up his hands for silence. After a moment, everyone quieted down.

"For the next four weeks, a small group of skaters will train here. Then we will have a competition."

"What kind of a competition?" someone called out.

Nikki strained her neck to see who had spoken up, but couldn't locate the voice.

Mr. Weiler held up his hands again. "Save your questions, please. There is someone here who can answer them better than I can. I'd like to introduce the head skating coach and coordinator of the Pennsylvania Special Olympics skating team, Sally Holmes."

The students burst into applause. An elegant-looking woman, her blond hair pulled back in a bun, stood up and faced the crowd.

"Hello," she said cheerfully.

"Hello!" Alex called back.

Everyone laughed. Nikki nudged Alex in the ribs, and Alex winked at her.

"Before you ask questions, I'd like to tell you about Special Olympics," said Ms. Holmes. "Special Olympics is a program of sports training and competition for people with mental retardation. Skating is just one of twenty-three sports in Special Olympics. We practice all year long, and we practice very hard."

"As hard as we do?" Nikki murmured to Jill.

Jill shrugged. "Sure, why not?" she whispered back.

"Unfortunately," Ms. Holmes continued, "this year we're having money problems. The ice rink where we usually practice was forced to close its doors. Mr. Weiler and Ms. Bart have graciously offered to let us use your rink during the morning hours. We usually have our own instructors, but the truth is, I think our skaters would really benefit from your coaching. After all, they too aspire to be Olympic athletes."

"Athletes?" a voice muttered. The question punched through the air like a cannonball.

Nikki couldn't believe it! She had been thinking the exact same thing. But she never would have said it out loud.

"Who said that?" Kathy demanded.

Sally Holmes glanced at Kathy and smiled calmly. "Wait, Kathy. It's an honest question. The answer is yes. Special Olympics participants *are* athletes. And yes, many people are uncomfortable around these athletes."

Nikki could feel the collective sigh as the group relaxed. But she was still tense about the whole thing. She wished the meeting were already over.

"There are a lot of things people don't understand about Special Olympics and the athletes who compete," Ms. Holmes continued. "It's true that some of them can barely stand on skates. But some of our skaters are quite good. We try to teach all our athletes that what's important is not winning, but achieving a personal best." Ms. Holmes paused dramatically and looked at the group with a twinkle in her eye. "But everyone likes to win!"

"Isn't 'Win, win, win' the Silver Blades cheer?" Tori said, giggling.

A murmur of laughter ran through the group. Most of them competed *only* to win.

"Okay, now the fun part!" Ms. Holmes said. "You all know how hard it is to find males who want to skate pairs. Well, we have the same problem in Special Olympics. So, some years back, Similar Pairs was invented. That's when two girls skate together as a pair."

She paused again. Then she nodded at someone, and the lights in the arena dimmed.

"And this year," Ms. Holmes continued, "we're introducing something new. There's a Special Olympics program called Unified Sports. It's a program that brings together athletes with and without mental retardation. They've started an event called Unified Similar Pairs—which means both of the skaters are the same sex, usually girls, and one of the skaters is a Special Olympics athlete, while one is not."

Without another word, Sally Holmes slid back into her seat.

A moment later Haley skated onto the ice, followed closely by Gabriella Nemo.

Nikki almost slid off the bleachers. Haley was going to do it—she was going to skate pairs with Gabriella!

As Nikki watched, the two girls reached the center of the rink and stopped. Haley reached out her hand to Gabriella. Then, slowly, the two glided around the rink, once and then twice. When they had gotten the feel of the ice—and of each other—Haley let go of Gabriella's hand.

They skated side by side, in perfect unison. Then they turned and skated backward, still perfectly side by side.

So what? Nikki wondered. I was doing that with my friends when I was five years old. She felt embarrassed. But she wasn't sure if she was embarrassed for Haley or for Gabriella or for both of them. She glanced at Jill to see if she was embarrassed, too. But Jill was leaning forward, watching intently.

Slowly but surely, Haley and Gabriella began their pairs routine. As the girls skated forward again their arms moved in perfect unison. Their left arms passed back as they glided forward with their left feet. Then their right arms swung forward as they skated forward with their right feet. Then, suddenly, both right legs passed in front, and they leaped into the air. Their landings were perfect. The crowd applauded.

A bunny hop? thought Nikki. Everyone is applauding a bunny hop?

But as Haley and Gabriella continued skating they remained in perfect harmony. Nikki had to admit that Gabriella was a very decent skater. She kept in unison with Haley. She did the jumps and turns cleanly. And the glow on her face was unmistakable. She loved to skate. Maybe almost as much as Nikki did. Still, she hadn't done anything very difficult.

And then, much to Nikki's surprise, she watched as the two skaters jumped from the outside edges of their forward left feet and did half a revolution in the air. They landed smoothly on their right outside edges. The crowd burst into applause as the two skaters bowed.

"Wow," said Alex. "I wouldn't have thought she could do a waltz jump."

"Me neither," said Nikki. "But it *is* a pretty simple jump."

She felt Alex glance at her. She knew he was sold on the idea of coaching the Special Olympics skaters. And it was clear that he was impressed with Gabriella. Nikki had to admit that she was impressed, too. But Gabriella was probably the best skater in this Special Olympics group. Why else had she been chosen for the demonstration? She was probably years ahead of the others. Nikki just knew that coaching the weaker skaters would be a giant waste of time.

"Okay," Ms. Holmes said enthusiastically as the lights came on. "Any questions now?"

Tori raised her hand. "I thought they needed more flourish at the end, and the part where they—"

"Hold on a second," Ms. Holmes said, cutting Tori off. "I didn't ask for criticism. I asked for questions."

"I don't understand," Tori complained. "Isn't the point to improve?"

"Yes, but remember, this was just a demonstration," Ms. Holmes said kindly.

Alex's hand shot up next. "Are you saying we shouldn't push the Special Olympics skaters the way we push each other?" he asked.

Ms. Holmes thought a moment before answering. "Not at all," she said finally. "This was a demonstration, not really a place for group criticism. But as far as your coaching goes, each skater is an individual and should be treated that way. Our skaters are on many different levels. Some of them are quite good and welcome criticism. Others can barely stand on the ice. You have to judge when to give positive criticism and when gentle encouragement would be better."

Before Nikki could stop herself, her hand went up in the air. "I don't understand," she heard herself say in a small voice. "How can someone who can barely stand up on the ice qualify to compete in Special Olympics?"

Ms. Holmes smiled. "That's a very good question," she said. "I know I said that anyone who wants to compete can. But they compete in an appropriate age and ability group."

"So someone can win a medal just for standing on the ice?" Tori asked, looking shocked.

"I know it's hard to understand," Ms. Holmes said. "But it's not quite as simple as that. Basically, we award badges to students who show they've learned something. Eventually they might move on to the kind of competition you're used to."

"How do we know what the skaters are capable of?"

"What if we push them too far?"

"What if they hurt themselves while we're teaching them something new?"

The questions followed in rapid succession. Ms. Holmes did her best to answer each one.

Nikki listened closely. It was a relief to discover that most of the others weren't sure how to deal with disabled people, either. And she was surprised to hear that some of her friends were afraid of seeming prejudiced. Some even admitted they were frightened.

But everyone seemed to want to do it, no matter how afraid or nervous they were. All of them, that is, except for Nikki. Nikki wondered what was wrong with her.

Finally Kathy ended the meeting. "Okay, people—time for you to get to school." As the group began to scatter, she added, "A sign-up sheet will be posted outside the pro shop. Those of you who want to volunteer, sign up! See you all at practice this afternoon."

As the skaters gathered their things, a buzz of excitement filled the air.

"See you later, Nik," Alex said. "I want to ask Ms. Holmes one more question."

Alex leaped up eagerly and raced to join the cluster of skaters forming around Sally Holmes. Nikki turned to ask Jill a question, but Jill and Tori were standing in the aisle, talking excitedly with Haley. Nikki hesitated. She needed to talk to someone. But she couldn't. What if there *was* something wrong with her? She was the only one not excited—by her own idea!

Nikki grabbed her skating bag and slipped past her friends. She had almost reached the front door when she heard Haley call her name. She pretended not to hear. Instead she pushed open the door and rushed outside.

3

As Nikki entered the Seneca Hills Ice Arena that afternoon, she felt as if her head were going to explode. Too many thoughts were competing for her attention. Why was she the only one who didn't want to coach a Special Olympics skater? How could she explain to her friends why she hadn't signed up?

All day long in school, she had tried to sort out her feelings. In between math problems and science experiments, she'd racked her brain. But it was no use. She didn't know why she felt the way she did.

Nikki was changing into her skates in the locker room when Haley entered, her face glowing with excitement.

"Hey, Nik," Haley greeted her friend as she opened her locker. She took out her skates, sat down next to

Nikki, and started to unlace her black combat boots. "Where'd you disappear to this morning?" she asked.

"Oh, I—uh—needed to finish some homework before school started," Nikki said.

"Math, huh?" Haley kicked off her boots.

"You were great this morning," said Nikki. "Nice skating."

"It was fun," said Haley. "Hey, are you coming to Super Sundaes this afternoon?"

"Sounds great." Nikki finished lacing up her skates. She loved going to the ice cream shop at the mall with her friends. They rarely went on weekdays. It would be a welcome break from the practice-school-practice-homework routine. She stuffed her belongings into her locker and closed the door.

"See you on the ice," she said to Haley.

"See you," said Haley. "Oh, listen, Gabriella is coming, too. She's bringing some of the Special Olympics skaters to meet us all this afternoon." Haley beamed. "Carrie can't wait to meet you."

"Carrie?" said Nikki. "Who's Carrie?"

"Haven't you checked the list Kathy posted? Carrie's the skater you're assigned to coach."

Nikki stared at Haley with a blank look on her face. "But I . . ."

"I know—you forgot to sign up!" Haley smiled. "All that math on your mind! Don't worry, I did it for you. I didn't want you to miss out."

Nikki took a deep breath and steadied herself. Haley

had signed her up? Nikki shook her head to clear it. She knew Haley was only trying to be a good friend.

"Didn't you want me to sign you up?" Haley asked.

Nikki swallowed hard. She was being ridiculous. Coaching a Special Olympics skater might even be fun. Maybe, if she was lucky, Carrie would be as good a skater as Gabriella.

"Sure, I wanted you to sign me up. It's fine," Nikki insisted. "I'm glad you did it."

"Oh, did I tell you? Gabriella's my partner," Haley said. "She's going to be great to work with. Especially when we skate Unified Similar Pairs—it's so much fun," Haley said. "Aren't you excited?"

Nikki felt a lump start to grow in her throat. She swallowed to force it down. "Yeah, it should be really fun for you and Gabriella."

"And for you and Carrie," Haley cried. "You're going to skate pairs, too. You and Carrie, me and Gabriella, and Martina and her partner, Lily. I hope we're all ready for the competition in just four weeks."

"Me too," Nikki said weakly. "Well, I've got to get to practice. See you later."

Nikki left the locker room in a fog. Behind her, she could hear Haley whistling happily as she finished lacing up her skates.

＞＜ ＞＜

The girls crowded through the mall entrance, talking a mile a minute. Nikki was grateful for the constant stream of chatter. Martina, Jill, Haley, and Tori were so busy talking, they didn't notice how quiet Nikki was. She wondered if she was the only one who was nervous.

"Hey—there they are!" Martina pointed at a group of girls lingering outside Super Sundaes.

As she followed the others to the cluster of girls, Nikki realized that she had expected them all to look like Gabriella. She had expected them to be the same age as Gabriella. She had even expected them to have the same disability as Gabriella. Which was what, exactly?

Nikki didn't know if Gabriella was retarded or not. And if she was, was it okay to call her retarded, or was there another word to use? Nikki glanced at her friends to see if any of them could tell how panicked she felt.

Meanwhile, Martina introduced the group of ten girls to one another. Nikki felt overwhelmed. She could barely look at Carrie, let alone talk to her. But at the moment it didn't seem to matter. In all the confusion, no one was paying any attention to Nikki. She was free to listen to the introductions.

Gabriella was the youngest of the Special Olympics skaters. A girl named Stacey, the skater assigned to Tori, was the oldest, at fifteen. Stacey was tall, with wide, friendly eyes and a little-girl voice. Nikki thought she was beautiful.

Twelve-year-old Lily was the exact opposite of Stacey. She was short and pudgy. When she opened her mouth to say hello, a raspy shout came out—along with a bubbly personality. Nikki watched Martina to see her reaction to Lily. Martina seemed thrilled with her new skating partner. She didn't seem at all embarrassed by how loudly Lily spoke.

Kendall, thirteen, had been assigned to Jill. A plain-looking girl, Kendall had a smooth speaking voice and a super sense of humor. In addition to having a mental disability, Kendall had a mild form of cerebral palsy. Nikki heard her telling Jill how she had learned how to skate with a leg brace. Jill listened to Kendall's story intently, with ease and fascination.

And then there was Carrie.

After one glance, Nikki felt she knew why Carrie was in Special Olympics. Carrie had the features of someone with Down syndrome. Her eyes were slightly slanted and puffy underneath. Nikki's heart sank. Why couldn't she have been paired with Kendall? Or even Stacey? Anyone with a less-obvious problem. She just wasn't sure how to deal with someone like Carrie.

But Haley quickly took over. She ushered everyone inside Super Sundaes and straight to the back of the restaurant, where a long, empty table awaited them.

"Okay—coaches on the right. Students, sit opposite your coach," Haley ordered.

"And I thought my *mother* was bossy!" Tori giggled nervously. Even Nikki had to laugh. Tori's mom was the pushiest stage mother she had ever met. Actually, Mrs. Carsen was probably the pushiest stage mom *any-*

one had ever met. She was a former figure skater herself, and she had big dreams for her daughter. Tori was a good skater, but never good enough for her mother.

Nikki found herself sandwiched between Jill and Tori. Haley was on Tori's other side, and Martina was at the very end of their table, next to Jill. Across the table sat Gabriella, Stacey, Carrie, Kendall, and Lily.

So far Carrie hadn't said a word. Nikki wondered if she could speak at all. She took a moment to look at her friends. But they were chattering away, getting to know their students.

Okay, Nikki told herself, give yourself a chance. Martina and Haley weren't new to this. They already knew Gabriella. But Tori wasn't acting very relaxed. In fact, she was acting as nervous as Nikki felt. She kept giggling like an idiot. And Tori was not a giggler. Nikki sighed. At least someone else was uncomfortable.

At her end of the table, Jill was talking so loudly she was practically yelling at poor Kendall. But at least they were trying. Nikki knew she wasn't giving Carrie a chance.

Just look at her and smile, Nikki told herself.

"Are you okay, Nikki?"

Nikki looked up, startled to find Carrie grinning at her, and noticed that Carrie's smile lit up her pretty face.

"Are you okay?" Carrie repeated. "You seem upset."

So I was wrong, thought Nikki. She can talk, and I am obviously freaked out.

"Um—I'm fine," Nikki said. "I was just thinking

about—um—about my baby brother. He's only five months old. Usually I only get to play with him after afternoon practice."

It was a weak excuse, and Nikki knew it. But if anyone else noticed, they were too polite to say anything.

"Oh, you have a five-month-old brother?" Kendall squealed. "My little cousin is five months old, too. He's so cute."

"I love babies," Carrie agreed.

Tori giggled nervously for what seemed like the hundredth time since they sat down.

Just then the waiter arrived. He carried the three Dreamboat Sundaes that Haley had ordered for everyone to split. He set two down on either end of the table. The last one went in the middle, directly between Nikki and Carrie. Carrie smiled impishly at Nikki.

"I love ice cream," she said, plunging her spoon into a mound of vanilla fudge ripple.

On either side of her, Nikki was aware that friendships were being forged over ice cream. One Dreamboat was being attacked by Haley, Gabriella, Tori, and Stacey, the other by Jill, Kendall, Martina, and Lily.

Carrie ate from the middle Dreamboat alone.

Nikki played with her spoon. Several times she raised it to take a spoonful of ice cream. But she just couldn't bring herself to share with Carrie. Silence hung over the two of them. There didn't seem to be anything she could do about it. And between Tori's giggling and Jill's shouting, she couldn't think straight.

"You can't catch it," Carrie said in a matter-of-fact tone.

Nikki stared at her. "What?"

"What I have. You can't catch it," Carrie repeated. She gestured at the Dreamboat with her spoon. She said it so openly that Nikki felt worse than ever.

"I just don't like ice cream," Nikki blurted. Then, to prove it, she flagged down the waiter and ordered a yogurt parfait. She ignored the stares of her friends, who knew she loved ice cream as much as any of them.

Haley polished off the last of the ice cream in front of her. "So," she said cheerfully. "Are we excited about this Unified Similar Pairs skating or what?"

A cheer rose up from Gabriella, Carrie, and Lily.

"I am sooooo excited," Carrie confessed to Nikki. She leaned over to scoop strawberry ice cream out of the sundae dish. As she did, her elbow knocked against a water glass. The glass went flying. Water spilled over the table and onto Carrie and Stacey. The other girls grabbed napkins and threw them their way.

Nikki tried not to gasp out loud. She couldn't believe it! Carrie was a klutz. She was totally clumsy! Plus, Carrie was sitting between Stacey and Kendall, and Nikki could see how small she was in comparison, despite being thirteen. Small and weak-looking. Nikki felt sick. She just knew that Carrie was one of those skaters who could barely stand on the ice.

"I saw you skate last year in the Silver Blades Ice Show," Carrie told Nikki calmly as she mopped up the water. "You and Alex Beekman. He's so cute. You were both really good."

Nikki nodded. Slowly she circled her spoon around the inside rim of the parfait glass. She gathered up the yogurt (which she didn't even like) and put it into her mouth.

"I was thinking," Carrie said. "Maybe we could do a waltz jump–loop jump combination at our competition."

"I don't think so," Nikki said as nicely as she could. How could anyone as clumsy as Carrie do a waltz jump–loop jump combination?

"I think it's a great idea!" Haley cried. She leaned over and yelled to Martina at the other end of the table. "Hey, Tina—what do you think about a waltz jump–loop jump for our Unified Similar Pairs competition?"

Martina's eyes sparkled as she looked at Lily. "What do you think, Lily? Can you handle it?"

"I can try!" Lily answered proudly.

"Are you sorry I'm not a pairs skater?" Kendall asked Jill.

Jill shook her head. "Absolutely not. I'm not a pairs skater myself," she said loudly.

"I'm not even a good skater," Kendall admitted.

"I'm probably not a good coach," Jill shouted.

"I'm not deaf either," said Kendall.

Jill's face turned several shades of red. Then she laughed. "Sorry," she said. "I guess I'm a little uncomfortable."

So am I, thought Nikki. Then she corrected herself. She was way more than just a little uncomfortable.

"How about it, Nikki? Can we try the waltz jump–loop jump?" Carrie asked eagerly.

Nikki looked at the small girl, so full of enthusiasm. She wished she could be equally enthusiastic.

"I guess so," was the best Nikki could manage. She stood up awkwardly and excused herself from the table. Hurrying into the ladies' room, she stayed there for a long time. When she came out, everyone was chipping in for the check. She paid her share and said goodbye to Carrie.

Tomorrow, she told herself. Tomorrow I'll be more used to the idea.

But she was convinced that the next day was when she would also see just how bad a skater Carrie really was.

4

"Nikki! Nikki, wake up!"

Nikki moaned and dived farther under the covers. She had been having the loveliest dream. She and Olympic skater Todd Sand were partnered at the Olympics and had just won a gold medal. A shower of rose petals had barely hit the ice when her mother's voice woke her up.

"Sorry, Mom," Nikki mumbled from underneath her quilt. "I guess I didn't hear the alarm go off."

"You didn't set your alarm, Nik," her mother said gently.

"What?" Nikki sat up in bed. "What time is it?"

"It's six o'clock, Nikki. I'm sorry. I would have woken you sooner, but I was up almost all night. Ben fell asleep at about four this morning."

Now Nikki was fully awake. "Why were you up all night with Ben? What's wrong with him?"

Nikki's mother sat down on the edge of the bed. "Nothing is wrong with him, Nikki. He's a baby. He was hungry, so he woke up. And then he thought it was time to play. I just had difficulty getting him back to sleep, that's all."

"Oh," Nikki said, relieved.

"I think the real question is, what's wrong with you?" her mom asked.

"What do you mean?" Nikki asked. "Why should anything be wrong with me?"

Mrs. Simon took a sip from the mug of coffee she had in her hands. "You've never forgotten to set your alarm before."

"I know," Nikki said. "And it will never happen again."

Her mother smiled. "And you're still in bed. The only other time you overslept you went crazy, racing around trying to get to the rink for five minutes of practice before school."

"You called me obsessed," said Nikki. "I'm trying to show you how levelheaded I can be."

"Really?" Her mother looked doubtful.

A loud wail came from down the hall. Mrs. Simon sighed.

"I'll get him, Mom." Nikki slid out from under the covers. "You stay here and have your coffee."

Her mother nodded gratefully. She sank back onto Nikki's bed. Nikki raced down the hall to her brother's room. Benjamin lay in his crib. His face was red from crying, and he was rocking from side to side.

"Hi, Benji." Tenderly, Nikki reached in and picked up the unhappy baby.

Benjamin laid his head against Nikki's chest. Nikki couldn't help wondering if her mother was wrong. Maybe there really was something wrong with him. Little babies shouldn't cry so much, should they?

Mrs. Simon appeared in the doorway. "Get dressed, Nikki. I'll take you to the rink. Your father already left."

"It's okay, Mom," said Nikki. "There really isn't time now. I'll skip morning practice and go straight to school. Why don't you go lie down again? I'll take care of Ben for a little bit."

Nikki knew that if her mother had slept the night before, they would now be in the middle of a why-didn't-you-set-your-alarm discussion. Not that it was necessary. Nikki knew why she hadn't. It was an accident. It really was.

Still, she had to admit that she didn't want to face the first day of coaching Carrie. She didn't want to see how bad a skater Carrie really was. And she didn't want to tell her that they couldn't possibly do a waltz jump–loop jump combination.

But Mrs. Simon was so exhausted that she didn't argue with Nikki at all. She just nodded and left the room. Nikki sat in the rocking chair with Ben. The baby stopped crying instantly. Nikki started humming, and within minutes Ben was asleep again. Nikki put him gently in his crib and went to check on her mother.

She was lying on top of her own bed, breathing softly. Nikki covered her with a blanket and went to get dressed.

As she searched through the pile of clothes on her chair for her favorite jeans, Nikki couldn't help going over the talk at the ice cream parlor. It bothered her that she was more nervous and upset than her friends. But something else bothered her, too. She didn't understand why her friends were encouraging hope where there wasn't any.

Why had Martina asked Lily if she could do a waltz jump–loop jump combination? No way could Lily do it. And why were her friends making such a big deal about the Unified Similar Pairs skating? They couldn't really be excited about it, could they?

Nikki squeezed herself into jeans and a powder blue sweater and ran down the hall to check on her brother again. She stood over the crib and stared at him. He looked so helpless. He *was* so helpless. He couldn't do anything for himself. As she stood there Nikki found herself wondering again how anyone would know if there was something wrong with Benjamin. When had Gabriella's mother known? Or Carrie's? As Nikki glanced at the baby she spotted one of her mother's baby books lying on the changing table. It was all about child development, describing the things tiny babies were supposed to do and when they were supposed to do them. Curious, she picked it up and sat down in the rocking chair to read.

After twenty minutes Nikki was totally panicked. She ran down the hall. "Mom! Mom, get up!" she cried.

"What's wrong?" Mrs. Simon sat straight up, suddenly wide awake.

Nikki waved the book in her mother's face. "You tell me, Mom. This book says Benji should be able to roll over already. He should be able to grasp things and do all kinds of things he can't do yet."

"Nikki, you can't believe everything you read. Those books provide general guidelines. Besides," she said, yawning, "he can do some of those things."

"Well, how would you know if there *was* something wrong with him?" Nikki said.

Mrs. Simon smiled gently. "Like what?" she asked.

"I don't know," Nikki mumbled. She took a deep breath. "Well, I mean, like—how would you know if he had Down syndrome?" she blurted.

Her mother eyed her levelly. "Benjamin doesn't have Down syndrome. We would have known right away. The doctor would have told us if there was anything wrong with him."

"Well, what if something bad happens to him when he's older?" Nikki went on. "I mean, how can you keep him safe?"

"Nothing is going to happen to Ben." Her mother smiled as she got up. "You sound just like a new mother," she commented. "Worried to death about your baby. It's true, honey—parents *do* want to keep their children safe. But you can't live that way, worried all the time. And what kid wants a parent hanging over them constantly, trying to keep them safe?"

Nikki thought about it. Her mother was right. She remembered when she was younger and how much she had wanted to be treated like a grown-up. She'd once had a big fight with her mom about crossing the street. Nikki had wanted to cross by herself, without holding someone's hand. Nikki had been only six years old, but she remembered that she had felt like a grown-up.

Nikki sighed. "Well, what do you do, then?" she asked.

Her mother smoothed Nikki's hair back with a gentle touch. "You try to teach kids how to take care of themselves. And then, when they're ready, you let them go. Let them take risks. After all, life is full of risks. But mostly people get through it just fine."

Nikki stared at her mom. She couldn't imagine tiny Ben ever being big enough to let go of. "I guess so," she mumbled.

Her mother looked at her quizzically. "Is this really about Ben? Or are you more worried about this girl from Special Olympics?"

Nikki was taken aback by the question. For a moment she couldn't answer. "Both, I guess," she finally said.

Her mother put an arm around her and gave her an affectionate squeeze. "Benjamin is fine, honey," she said. "And this girl Carrie may have Down syndrome, but my guess is that she's fine, too. She obviously has someone to love her and look out for her. And to encourage her to skate. That's a risk, too, isn't it? It almost seems as if you're the one with the problem. Exactly what are you so scared of?"

"I don't know," Nikki admitted.

"Well, instead of spending all your time worrying about Ben, why don't you think about that question?" Mrs. Simon kissed Nikki on the cheek. "Now let's go get some breakfast."

The first thing Nikki did at the Ice Arena that afternoon was to go straight to Kathy Bart's office.

"I'm sorry I missed practice this morning," she said to her coach.

Kathy shrugged, her nose buried in the paperwork on her desk. "You're talking to the wrong person," she said. "For the next four weeks, you're the coach. Carrie is your student and your partner. Apologize to her."

"Don't you want to know what happened?" Nikki asked.

Kathy looked up. "I don't want to be cruel, Nikki. But this is part of learning to be a good coach. It doesn't matter what happened. You should have found a way to let Carrie know you wouldn't be here."

"Oh," said Nikki quietly. She turned to leave the office.

"Wait. You're okay, aren't you?" Kathy asked.

Nikki turned and smiled. "Yeah. Thanks for asking," she said.

Kathy smiled back. "Good. Then I'll see you on the ice in five minutes."

Twenty minutes later, though, Kathy wasn't smiling anymore. "Try it again," she called in a tired voice.

Nikki took a deep breath. She glided toward Alex on her left leg. Her right leg was extended behind her. The lesson was going poorly. Nikki couldn't keep her mind off Carrie and what Kathy had said, what her mother said, and . . .

Concentrate, she told herself again. Focus on the move.

Alex took her hand. Focus on Alex, she thought. Does he have a good grasp on your hand? Are you in the right position? Don't think so much. Just . . . one, two, three—

Alex's hands circled firmly around her waist. Nikki arched her back as she was lifted up and turned. Then, suddenly, she was lying flat on the ice. Alex was sprawled beside her.

Nikki groaned as she sat up. "What happened?" she asked.

"You were way overarched," Kathy said, skating over to them. "Alex couldn't balance you."

"You're kidding!" Nikki felt surprised.

"You don't believe me?" Kathy asked.

"Of course I believe you," Nikki told her coach. "It's just that beginners overarch. Not me."

"Unless you're not concentrating," Kathy said.

The rest of the lesson was a disaster. No matter how hard she tried, Nikki just couldn't seem to focus on her skating. By the time her mother picked her up, Nikki knew one thing for sure: She had to accept Carrie and the fact that she was supposed to coach her, or else her own skating was going to suffer.

The next morning Nikki awakened to a medley of golden oldies from the sixties. The music was loud enough to wake the entire neighborhood. But still Nikki couldn't get out of bed. Her stomach felt fluttery. She just wasn't ready to face Carrie. She'd have to miss practice again. But she needed an excuse this time. And she needed to get in touch with Carrie, too.

Nikki dragged herself out of bed and went downstairs to the kitchen. She dialed Haley's number.

"What's up?" Haley's cheerful voice answered the phone.

"I have a really bad headache. I can't go to morning practice," Nikki told her.

"Sorry you have a headache. But why are you telling me?" Haley wanted to know.

"I don't have Carrie's number. Could you call her for me?"

"Yeah. Okay," Haley said. "And I'll get you her number, too. Feel better."

The dial tone echoed in Nikki's ear. Was it her imagination, or had Haley practically hung up on her?

Nikki went to her room and dived back under the covers. A few minutes later, her mother came in.

"Oh, Nikki, not again!" her mother cried.

"I'm really not feeling well, Mom," Nikki insisted.

Her mother said nothing. At least she said nothing

then. But that afternoon, as Mrs. Simon stopped the car in front of the skating rink, she had plenty to say.

"Nikki, I want you to know that it's natural for you to be nervous about coaching Carrie."

"I know, Mom." Nikki opened the car door to get out.

"I don't think you do know," her mother said, laying a hand on her arm. "Honey, it's normal to worry about doing something new. But you'll never get over your fears if you don't try. You committed yourself, so you can't just avoid coaching someone who's disabled. So now give it a try. Watch Carrie skate. Get to know her. You might be surprised."

"By her skating?" Nikki asked. "You think she might really be good?"

"I have no idea how her skating will be. I just meant that you might be surprised by Carrie herself. After all, you've never met anyone like her before. You might enjoy working with her. You might even *like* her. At least, give her a chance."

Nikki stared at her mother. I might like her? she repeated to herself. I might like her? A million thoughts swarmed through her brain. "Mom," she exclaimed, "you're a genius! Thanks a lot!"

Her mother stared in surprise as Nikki slammed the car door and hurried toward the rink. This wouldn't be easy, Nikki knew, but even so, she felt more cheerful than she had in days.

5

Nikki skated much better than she had the day before. Nevertheless, she couldn't wait to be done. The instant practice was over, Nikki hurried into the locker room. Haley was already there, lacing her boots over tie-dyed tights. Her tousled hair hung down over her face.

"Hi, Haley!" Nikki sat down on the bench next to her.

"Hi, Nikki," Haley said softly.

Nikki sighed. "Listen, I know you're mad at me. Probably everyone is mad at me."

"Carrie isn't," Haley said. "Not much, at least. She understands."

"She does?" asked Nikki, surprised.

"Better than I do," said Haley. She looked up, tucking her hair behind her ears. "I'm not mad. Well, I'm a little mad. But I'm also worried about you. What's going on?"

"I wasn't sure at first," said Nikki. "But I think I know now. And I was hoping you would talk to me about it."

Haley shrugged. "Sure. Talk. Only I have to leave in a few minutes. I'm going to the mall with Martina."

"Really?" Nikki was surprised. "I didn't know you and Martina were such good friends."

"We aren't yet," said Haley. "But I've been spending a lot of time around her since I started coaching Gabriella. I really like her. I like them both."

"You like Gabriella as a friend?" Nikki asked cautiously.

"Yeah. Why? Don't you like Carrie?"

Nikki studied Haley for a minute before answering. She watched as Haley tied her hair up in a ponytail.

"I guess I don't know Carrie," she admitted. "I don't know if I like her or not. Look, Haley, that's what I wanted to talk to you about. The truth is that I've never actually met a—a—" Nikki searched for the right word.

"A person with Down syndrome?" Haley asked directly.

"A person who's retarded in *any* way," Nikki admitted.

"Ever?" Haley's eyes were wide with surprise.

"Ever," said Nikki. "Have you? I mean before you met Gabriella?"

Haley nodded. "Sure."

Nikki opened her locker. She pulled out her cowboy boots and sat down on the bench to unlace her skates.

She could feel Haley staring at her, but she couldn't think of what to say.

"Before I moved here I lived in a really small town," Nikki said finally. "Everyone knew everyone, and everyone was pretty much the same. I guess Carrie kind of scares me."

"Hey, Haley, let's go!" Martina burst in through the locker room door. When she saw Nikki, she paused awkwardly. "Oh. Hi, Nikki."

"Hi, Martina," Nikki said, a wave of embarrassment coming over her.

Martina, hesitated, frowning. "Listen, Nikki," she finally said, "I guess I should tell you that Carrie is a little upset that you haven't shown up for any of the practices."

"She's upset?" Nikki asked. Despite what Haley had said, Nikki had secretly hoped Carrie wasn't really feeling hurt.

"Sure she is," Martina said. "She's only human. You stood her up twice."

Nikki stared at Martina helplessly. Haley grabbed Martina's arm.

"Better have a seat, Tina," Haley told her. "Nik here has a problem she needs to talk to you about."

Nikki felt her face flush. Was Haley crazy? No way was she going to talk to Martina about this. Gabriella was her sister—and she was mentally retarded!

"Go ahead," said Haley. "Tell her what you told me."

Nikki shook her head and leaned over to unlace her skates.

"Okay, then *I'll* tell her." Haley looked at Martina. "Nikki's never met a person with retardation before," she said bluntly.

Nikki was alarmed that Haley had blurted out her secret. At the same time, she was amazed that Haley was so comfortable about it. Still, she was afraid to look at Martina.

But Martina didn't get angry at all. "No kidding?" Martina said. "I don't think I ever did, either—until Gabriella was born."

Nikki felt every muscle in her body suddenly relax. "Really?" she asked.

"Really."

To Nikki's surprise, all her fears suddenly came pouring out. She told Martina and Haley how she'd worried about meeting Carrie. How she'd even started to worry about Benjamin.

"I feel so much better, telling you all this," she said to Martina. "You can't believe how worried I was. I kept thinking, what if Ben has Down syndrome? Or what if—" Suddenly she stopped. "Oh, I'm sorry," she gasped. She had practically told Martina that she was afraid Ben would turn out like Gabriella!

"It's okay," Martina said quickly. "I know exactly how you feel."

"You do?" Nikki was shocked. And relieved!

Martina nodded. "When Javier was born, I remember standing over his crib and wondering if he was going to be like Gabriella. So I know how you feel."

"Javier?" Haley asked in confusion. "Who's he?"

"My younger brother," Martina said, laughing. "There are six of us. Javier was born after Gabriella."

"And is he . . ." Nikki couldn't finish the sentence.

Martina smiled. "No, he isn't," she said. "He's four years old and he's probably smarter than all of us put together." She beamed proudly at Nikki and Haley. "Anyway," she continued, "let me tell you a story." Martina took a deep breath.

"One day," she said, "when Javier was about two months old, I was staring at him while he was sleeping. I couldn't help wondering if he was going to be like Gaby. I felt really guilty, thinking that way. Then all of a sudden, Gabriella came into the room and stood next to me. And she looked at him and said, 'He won't be like me, will he?' I said, 'What if he is?' and she said, 'It will be easier for him if he isn't.' " Martina paused.

"Wow," Nikki said softly.

Martina put her hand on Nikki's arm. "So don't sell Carrie short, either. She probably understands a whole lot more than you think she does."

"I don't know what to say," Nikki answered.

"Hey, I've got an idea! Gabriella asked Carrie to dinner at my house tomorrow night," Martina said. "Why don't you come, too? It'd be a great chance to talk to Carrie, to get to know her before you coach her."

"Won't Carrie know we planned it?" Nikki asked.

Martina grinned at her. "See? You're already treating Carrie like she has some common sense. That's a great start."

Nikki grinned, too. "It's a perfect idea!"

"Haley, why don't you come also?" Martina asked.

"Okay with me," said Haley.

"Let me check with my mom," Martina said. "But I'm sure it'll be okay. With eight people in our family, there's always tons of food around!" Martina glanced at her watch. "And speaking of tons of food, if we don't get to the mall now, Haley, I'll never make it home in time for dinner."

Haley finished dressing and stood up.

Martina turned to Nikki. "I'll see you tomorrow about seven, okay? If there's a problem, I'll let you know."

"I can't wait," Nikki said. And she meant it.

6

The inside of the Nemo house was like nothing Nikki had ever seen before. In one way, it kind of reminded her of Jill's house—there were so many kids around. But there was also something different. The whole place was filled with a special kind of comfortable, homey feeling. And then there were the smells—delicious, mouthwatering smells coming from the kitchen. They weren't familiar, but they were wonderful.

And it was the way the house was decorated. Nikki searched her mind for the right word and decided on *ornate,* meaning very fancy and decorated. The vocabulary word had won her first prize in her fifth-grade spelling bee. Nikki thought the Nemos' house was a really unusual combination, cozy and ornate at the same time.

Martina's mother was a tall, slender woman with auburn hair, dark eyes, and a warm, wonderful smile. Nikki liked her instantly.

"Glad you could come, Nikki," Mrs. Nemo told her before hurrying back off to the kitchen.

"Wow! Does your mom spend all day cooking?" Nikki whispered to Martina.

"Nah. She works," said Martina. "Full-time."

"Really?" asked Nikki. "When does she do all the cooking?"

"She doesn't. She's just helping Dad today. Mom's a partner in a law firm. My dad stays home with us."

"Really?" Nikki's mouth dropped open and her eyes went wide.

Martina laughed. "Sure. Haven't you heard of families like that before?"

Nikki shook her head.

"Poor Nikki." Haley patted her friend on the shoulder. "She's been living in a cave."

Now Nikki laughed, but the comment made her uncomfortable. Had she been living in a cave? Didn't she know what the rest of the world was like?

"Dinner!" someone bellowed from the kitchen.

Nikki joined the flow of children into the dining room. The table was set for eleven: six Nemo kids and two parents, plus Haley, Nikki, and Carrie.

Nikki glanced quickly around the spacious room. "My family only eats in the dining room for fancy occasions," she whispered to Haley as they slid into their seats.

"Mine too!" Haley whispered back loudly.

Gabriella, who had seated herself on the other side of Nikki, leaned over.

"We can't all fit around the kitchen table," she said, giggling. "So we have to eat in the dining room."

Nikki gazed thoughtfully at the loud, happy family. Javier and Gabriella were reaching for food before they were even seated. Then four-year-old Javier started pushing his chair in and out. Martina's older brother leaned over to scold him. Nikki had already forgotten his name . . . and the name of Martina's older sister. The teenage girl looked like an adult to Nikki as she bustled around the table, making sure everyone had water to drink. In the middle of that, she leaned over and strapped the baby into his high chair. Everyone was so busy, but relaxed.

Martina set a steaming platter of some sort of chicken dish on the table in front of the baby. His chubby hand reached out for the hot plate. Nikki was about to warn someone, but Gabriella saw and moved the hot dish away. Nikki couldn't help smiling. It was probably the craziest family scene—and the happiest— she had ever been a part of.

Not that her own family wasn't happy. It was, she reminded herself. But until five months ago, it had just been Nikki and her parents. She still wasn't used to having a brother around. She wasn't used to sharing all the attention. But none of the Nemo kids seemed to have trouble sharing the spotlight. Far from it. They all seemed to feel important and included. It really seemed as if they were having fun.

And Gabriella, sitting next to Nikki, was as much a part of the fun as the rest of the family.

When the hustle and bustle finally settled down, Nikki realized that Carrie was sitting directly across the table from her.

Nikki took a deep breath. "Hi, Carrie," she said shyly.

Much to Nikki's surprise, the girl's face lit up. "Hi, Nikki! How are you feeling?" Carrie asked.

"Um—I'm fine." Nikki felt ashamed at the lies she had been telling. "My headache's gone now."

"So," boomed a male voice, "everybody dig in." Nikki stared at Mr. Nemo. She couldn't believe he had cooked the entire feast sitting before them. Her own father could hardly boil an egg.

Everyone began eating. The food tasted great—as good as it smelled. But Nikki was aware of Carrie watching her, studying her, and it made her uncomfortable.

"So," Mr. Nemo boomed again. Nikki wondered if he began every sentence with *so*.

"How's the commute going, Carrie?" he asked.

Carrie looked at Mr. Nemo and smiled. "Oh, great!" she said. "I love to get up before the sun."

Everyone laughed. But Nikki was confused. "Why do you get up before the sun?" she asked Carrie.

"I live in Winchester Falls. I get up at four and eat breakfast, then my mom drives me to the bus stop."

"You get up at *four*?" Nikki couldn't believe it! Did Carrie really love skating that much? She hadn't given her nearly enough credit. Nikki knew she should apologize to Carrie, but before she could get the words out, Mr. Nemo's voice bellowed across the table again.

"So, girls—how is practice going?"

"Yes, and how are your new coaches?" Mrs. Nemo added, her eyes twinkling.

"Great!" Gabriella answered. "Haley and I are working on the waltz jump–loop jump combination." She smiled impishly. "We're going to beat Martina and Lily at the competition!"

"In your dreams," Martina answered, grinning at her from across the table.

"We'll have to watch out for Nikki and Carrie, too," Haley said.

Nikki knew that Haley was just trying to be helpful, but the comment made her feel worse than she did already. She looked down at her food, afraid to meet Carrie's eyes. But when she finally had the courage to look up, Carrie was smiling happily, enjoying the friendly banter around her. Nikki was stunned. Carrie had gotten up twice at a ridiculous hour in the morning to practice with a partner who hadn't shown up. If she was angry, she wasn't letting on.

Nikki couldn't say a word for the rest of the meal. Luckily no one noticed—there were so many other conversations going on, sometimes all at once.

After dinner everyone pitched in to clear the dishes.

Then Nikki and Haley helped Martina fill the dishwasher. By the time they were done, the rest of the kids had scattered all over the house.

"Want to see my room?" Martina asked Nikki.

"Um, sure, but I have something to do first," Nikki told Martina and Haley. Her two friends exchanged a knowing look.

"Is it about Carrie?" Haley asked.

Nikki nodded. "Yeah. I didn't realize how serious she is about practicing. I guess I really owe her an apology."

Martina nodded, and Haley clapped Nikki on the back. "Great idea," Haley said. "Come find us afterward. And good luck!"

Nikki had to search for Carrie and Gabriella. Finally she found them in the family room. Both girls were jumping up and down, their arms making wide circles. Nikki was startled for a moment. Then she realized they were watching an aerobic-dance video and following the instructions. Nikki stood in the doorway and looked on.

"I love this part coming up," said Gabriella, panting.

"Me too," Carrie said. Both girls switched to a side-to-side sliding motion. Carrie's movements were jerky rather than smooth, though. "It's just like skating!" she called out.

Oh, no! Nikki thought. I hope she skates better than she dances!

Gabriella noticed Nikki standing in the doorway. "Come dance," she said. "It's fun."

Nikki shook her head. "No, thanks."

"Don't you like to dance?" Carrie asked.

"Sure," said Nikki. "But for fun, not as exercise."

Carrie laughed. "That's what Steve says."

"Who?" Nikki asked politely.

"Steve is her boyfriend," Gabriella explained.

"Ooh! Ooh! This is my favorite part!" Carrie squealed as the TV showed a grapevine step. Both girls started doing it, moving across the floor and back again, over and over.

Nikki was stunned. Carrie had a boyfriend? Every new thing she learned about Carrie was unexpected and impressive.

She woke up at four to skate.

She loved to dance.

Haley was right. Nikki *had* been living in a cave.

She would watch Carrie skate and give her the benefit of the doubt . . . even if she was a pretty lousy aerobics dancer.

"Carrie—would you like to practice together tomorrow morning?" Nikki blurted out.

"Tomorrow is Sunday." Carrie giggled. She and Gabriella were ready to begin the cool-down. "Besides," Carrie said as she hung over her knees, "maybe you aren't a good partner for me."

"What?" Nikki cried before she could stop herself. Was Carrie kidding? It had never occurred to Nikki that Carrie might not want *her* as a partner.

Carrie and Gabriella finished their cool-down with a

salute to the sun. Gabriella turned off the videotape, then slid quietly out of the room.

A long, uncomfortable silence followed Gabriella's exit. Finally Nikki spoke.

"Look, Carrie, I'm sorry I missed those two practices," she said. "But things came up."

Carrie looked directly at her. "Did they?" she asked simply.

Nikki opened her mouth to defend herself. But Carrie spoke again.

"It's okay," she said. "Lots of people are not comfortable around me."

Nikki felt her cheeks flame. Then her lips relaxed into a smile. "Give me a chance, okay?" she said. "Tomorrow morning at ten?"

"Okay," Carrie said.

Nikki smiled, and hurried to find Martina and Haley. She couldn't wait to tell them she had finally done the right thing.

～ ～

When Nikki got home that night she found a message that Danielle Panati had called. Nikki dialed the number from memory.

"Danielle, how are you? We miss you at the rink!" Nikki cried into the phone. She saw her friend at school, but somehow it wasn't the same as it used to be.

"I miss you guys, too," Danielle said.

Danielle had been a member of Silver Blades until she decided that ice-skating was taking up too much of her time. Now she skated just for fun. Her new passion was the school newspaper.

"So, how's the star reporter for the *Grandview Gazette*?" Nikki asked.

"Snooping, as usual," Danielle said, laughing. "Which is why I'm calling, actually. I hear Silver Blades is hosting a Special Olympics event. I wanted to interview you about it."

Nikki felt her stomach churn slightly. But she dismissed it as a result of having eaten too much of the Nemo feast. "Sure. What do you want to know?"

"Well, what's it like?" Danielle asked.

"What's what like?"

"Nikki, is this a bad time?" Danielle always knew when there was something wrong.

"No." Nikki sighed. "Nothing's wrong. I just haven't had a chance to do any coaching yet. I guess you should call back in a couple of days."

"Why don't I just stop by the rink next week, okay?" Danielle said eagerly.

"Okay," Nikki agreed.

Nikki had to smile to herself. Clearly Danielle was going to be as disciplined a reporter as she had been an ice-skater. But what was she going to see when she stopped by the ice rink?

What if Carrie turned out to be a really horrible

skater? What if she hurt herself while they were practicing? What if . . . Nikki sighed and reached for her
alarm clock. It was time to stop being fearful. It was
time to keep her promise to Carrie. She was definitely
going to show up the next morning. She couldn't let
Carrie down again.

7

"What on earth is going on?" Mrs. Simon said as she entered Nikki's room Sunday morning.

"Sorry, Mom." Nikki reached over and shut off the alarm clock on top of her dresser. A faint, high-pitched beeping still sounded from somewhere in the room. Nikki dived under her bed and pulled out the watch she had borrowed from her dad the night before. She fumbled with it before remembering how to shut off the alarm.

Nikki smiled sheepishly as she held the watch out to her mother. "Could you give this to Dad when he wakes up?"

"Sure," Mrs. Simon said. "You're really going to meet Carrie at the rink this morning?"

Nikki nodded. "Yep. I practiced my poker face last

61

night. How is it?" Nikki made her face as neutral as she could and looked at her mom.

"It's great, honey. But why do you need a poker face?"

"I watched Carrie dancing last night. And if I had any hope at all that she could skate, well . . ."

"Remember, just give her a chance, honey."

"I will, Mom, I will."

∼ ∕

The Seneca Hills Ice Arena was more crowded than Nikki had ever seen it. She guessed it was because colder weather was approaching. People were digging their old ice skates out of the garage and getting ready for winter sports. For a minute Nikki regretted meeting Carrie during a public skate session. The ice was already pretty chopped up, and the rink was packed with bad skaters. There was a greater chance of an accident and a greater chance that Carrie might get hurt. They should have waited until Monday morning.

Nikki glanced at the large clock on the wall. It was only 9:45. She had told Carrie to meet her at ten by the bleachers. Nikki had already done her warm-up stretches at home. That gave her just enough time to do a couple of warm-up laps. Then she would head for the center of the rink and practice her double Lutz. She had been having so much trouble with it lately that she wanted extra time to work on it.

Nikki skated her warm-up laps, weaving in and out

and around skaters of all levels. She became aware of a skater in the center of the rink drawing a lot of attention. Nikki saw a blur of motion that she recognized as the end of a spin. She knew by the skating skirt that the skater was a girl. She was good, really good. And she was skating on the only part of the entire rink that wasn't too chopped up to practice spins on. Nikki felt a wave of disappointment. Now she would never get to practice her triple! Oh, well. She looked back toward the bleachers. Maybe Carrie had arrived.

"Nikki!"

Nikki turned in the direction of the voice calling her name. Even as she saw the hand rise and start to wave, she knew that it was Carrie calling. What she couldn't believe was that Carrie was the girl in the center of the rink—the girl who had just performed the beautiful spin.

Nikki's heart soared with hope. Could Carrie be as good a skater as the spin seemed to prove? She forced herself to calm down. A lot of people could do one thing really well.

Nikki skated over to Carrie, her mind racing. What should she say? She tried to imagine what her coach, Kathy, would say, or what Haley would say to Gabriella. But nothing came to mind.

She reached Carrie and stopped, spraying little shavings of ice everywhere.

"Hi, Carrie. I didn't see you. How long have you been here?" Nikki asked pleasantly.

"You didn't see me?" Carrie was visibly disappointed.

Nikki felt weird, but she had already messed up so much with Carrie. She wanted to be very careful from now on.

"Let's see what you can do," Nikki said cheerfully.

"What do you want to see?" Carrie asked.

Nikki shrugged. "Is there a routine you've worked on?" she asked.

Carrie nodded eagerly.

"Let's see it!" Nikki tried to sound both enthusiastic and in command at the same time. She knew she needed to sound like a real coach.

Nikki backed onto some of the choppy ice so Carrie would have more room. She waited, holding her breath. She really hoped that the spin was a taste of more to come and not Carrie's only good move.

Carrie started off slowly, skating forward and then backward in a wide circle. She was graceful and fluid, not at all like the awkward dancer Nikki had seen the night before!

Nikki held her breath as Carrie moved into a spin, arching her back. Carrie's arms were perfectly positioned at her sides. As she spun faster and faster she brought them smoothly in front of her. Nikki watched her face. It glowed with joy. Carrie was truly a skater.

The rest of the routine was beautiful, though not without mistakes. Carrie finished with a flourish. Nikki searched her mind for the best way to respond. Should she congratulate or criticize? But in the end the words seemed to come out all by themselves.

"Carrie—that was great!" Nikki said.

"You don't have to look so surprised," Carrie said playfully.

"I-I'm sorry," Nikki stammered. "I just didn't expect you to be this good."

"I know," Carrie said proudly. "Now tell me what I did wrong."

At that instant Nikki realized that this was the part of coaching that frightened her the most. She had no idea how Carrie would respond to criticism. Carrie was so good that it made Nikki want to push her even harder. Inside, she was bursting with excitement. They might have a chance to win the competition! More than anything, Nikki loved winning.

"Hey, you guys!" Tori called as she skated up to Nikki and Carrie.

"Hi, Tori." Nikki was relieved to have a few more minutes to decide how to act with Carrie.

"I heard everyone had dinner without me last night," Tori teased.

"Pairs skaters only," Carrie said, giggling.

Nikki found herself giggling, too. "Yeah. Pairs skaters only," she echoed.

"I know. Haley told me." Tori smiled. "Hey—come over and see Stacey."

"Where is she?" Nikki asked.

"She's holding on to the railing over there." Tori gestured toward Stacey, who was slipping from side to side even as she clung to the railing. Still, she had a determined look on her face.

Nikki and Carrie followed Tori over to the struggling girl.

"Hey, Stace, let's show them what you've learned so far!" Tori said. "Wait till you see this," she added in a proud whisper.

Nikki watched as the tall, pretty girl let go of the side of the rink. She took four awkward, wobbly glides forward, turned, skated two steps backward, and fell.

"That was great!" Tori cried. She skated over to help Stacey up.

"But I fell again," Stacey moaned.

"I know, but this time you turned before you fell," Tori told her.

Nikki couldn't believe it. Was this the Tori Carsen she knew? The bossy, competitive Tori Carsen? The Tori who had once stolen a training tape so Nikki couldn't watch it?

Nikki watched for a few more minutes as Tori patiently coached Stacey. Sometimes she said "Great!" in a loud, exuberant voice. Sometimes she used a quiet, reassuring "That was fine" or "Nice try." Watching her, Nikki decided the latter approach was the one she should take with Carrie.

"Ready to try some pairs skating?" she said, turning to Carrie. "We've got a competition to get ready for!"

Carrie's eyes glistened as she nodded.

"Let's go back to the center of the rink, where it's less chopped up," Nikki suggested.

Nikki and Carrie skated side by side. Nikki talked her new partner through a series of moves, saying "Fine,

fine" over and over. Carrie caught on quickly, and she executed some of the moves well. But she had never skated pairs before, and her timing was off. Nikki held back the urge to criticize her, remembering how Tori had been with Stacey. But then Carrie messed up a simple move.

"You aren't counting properly," Nikki told Carrie. "Watch me."

Carrie stood on the ice, her eyes riveted on Nikki. Nikki counted out loud rhythmically while she skated backward.

"One and two and turn and turn and watch my arms and jump and turn." Nikki finished the move and smiled. "Ready to try it?"

"Yes," Carrie said.

She started the same way Nikki had, and counted out loud just as she had watched Nikki do. But when Carrie got to the jump, her arms were in the wrong position, and that threw her off balance. She stumbled and fell.

Nikki flew to her side.

"Carrie, are you all right?" she cried.

"I'm okay." Carrie sat up and rubbed her knee. "Let's try it again."

"No," Nikki said, her heart pounding. "That's the end of the lesson. We'll try again tomorrow."

"I'm not hurt," Carrie protested. "Just one more try."

"It's late. We've already skated a long time. I have to go," Nikki said. She felt terrible! She shouldn't have criticized her. Carrie could have gotten hurt, and it would have been all Nikki's fault. She wouldn't make that mistake again. The next time, all she would say was "Fine."

Winning was one thing. But pushing a girl like Carrie too hard was something Nikki never wanted to do. She'd just have to back off. No matter what, she couldn't let Carrie get hurt.

Nikki kept her promise to herself. On Monday morning she ignored every one of Carrie's mistakes. She kept saying "Fine, fine" as if that was the only word she knew.

Tuesday morning she did the same thing. They finished by practicing a required move for the upcoming competition. Carrie's timing was off again. But Nikki said it looked fine and left it at that.

Behind them, Haley and Gabriella glided across the ice in perfect harmony. Haley counted out loud as Nikki had, but she also called out pointers to Gabriella. It took some effort for Nikki to ignore the other pair but so far she was pulling it off.

Carrie gazed at Haley and Gabriella and sighed. "What am I doing wrong?" she asked Nikki.

"What?"

"I must be doing *something* wrong," Carrie repeated. "Tell me."

"No," said Nikki. "You're doing fine."

"What about my timing?" Carrie persisted. "I know it's off."

Nikki longed to agree. She longed to point out everything Carrie was doing wrong—not because she wanted to be critical, but because she knew Carrie was a good skater who could be even better. Maybe even as good as Gabriella. Nikki longed to push Carrie to her limits, just to see how good she could be. To see if there was a chance they could win the competition. But every time she thought about the fall Carrie had taken on Sunday, she got nervous.

"You're doing your best," Nikki said. "That's what counts."

When Nikki arrived at the Seneca Hills Ice Arena on Wednesday morning, she was surprised to see the ice smooth and untouched. Usually the Special Olympics skaters arrived a few minutes earlier and warmed up. Nikki glanced at the large clock that hung on the wall. She was early. Maybe she could get in a little practice on her double Lutz. It would be great to have the whole rink to herself.

But when she entered the locker room Nikki heard voices. She recognized Carrie's instantly.

"She's a very nice person. She just isn't a good coach."

"Why isn't she good?" Nikki recognized Gabriella's voice.

"She always says what I do is fine," Carrie answered. "But I know that's not true." She paused. "Do you think Sally would give me a new partner?"

"She might. But Nikki is a great pairs skater," Gabriella said. "You've seen her skate, remember?"

"I know she is," Carrie agreed.

"And you want to skate pairs," Gabriella said.

"Yeah," Carrie agreed.

Then there was silence. Nikki assumed they were about to leave the locker room. She didn't want to be discovered eavesdropping, so she began to whistle and walked into view.

"Good morning," Gabriella called to her as she quickly left the room. Carrie finished lacing her skates and stood up to leave, too.

"See you on the ice," she said to Nikki.

"Wait!" Nikki called after Carrie. "Is there something you want to talk about?"

Carrie turned quickly.

"What?" She looked as if she'd been caught doing something wrong.

"It's all right, Carrie," Nikki said gently. "I heard you and Gabriella talking. If you want to get a new coach, that's okay with me. But will you just tell me why?"

Carrie shifted uneasily from foot to foot but said nothing. Finally Nikki went to her locker and opened it.

"Have you seen how good Haley and Gabriella are?" Carrie blurted out.

"Yes," Nikki said softly without turning around.

"Have you seen Martina and Lily?"

"Yes," said Nikki. "But I don't think they're as good as Haley and Gabriella."

"But they might be," said Carrie. "They practice a lot."

Nikki turned and looked at Carrie. "We're practicing," she said.

Carrie giggled. "You're practicing—practicing saying 'Fine' over and over."

Nikki laughed. "I guess I do say that word a lot," she admitted.

"You sure do," Carrie said.

An uncomfortable silence followed. Nikki sat on the bench and began pulling on her skates.

"Don't you want to win?" Carrie asked suddenly.

Nikki was surprised by the question. "Are you kidding? I live to win! My mother says I'm obsessed with winning."

"Then what's the problem?" Carrie asked. "I like to win, too."

Nikki took a deep breath. "I don't want you to get hurt," she admitted.

"Me neither," Carrie said.

Nikki smiled. She was getting used to, even fond of, Carrie's way of cutting right to the point.

"It *would* be really nice to win that competition," she said, trying to be as honest as Carrie.

"It would." Carrie's eyes gleamed. "Don't you think we're good enough?"

"Well . . . not right now," Nikki said truthfully.

"But could we be?" Carrie asked.

Nikki nodded. "We could be," she said slowly.

"So . . . ," Carrie began.

"So what?" Nikki said.

"So why won't you try?"

"I just don't know how to coach you," Nikki admitted. "I watched what Tori was doing. She says 'Fine' and 'Great' to Stacey, and it works—uh—fine."

They both laughed.

"It does," Carrie said. "But Stacey can't even stand up on skates. I can!"

Nikki thought about it. "What should I do?" she asked.

"Do what Haley does. Give me pointers. Count with me. Teach me to skate pairs," Carrie said.

Nikki finished lacing her skates, stood up, and walked over to Carrie.

"Okay. Let's do it!" she said. "Let's skate to win!"

Carrie let out a cheer. "All right!" she shouted.

They left the locker room together and headed straight for the ice rink. It was time for them to become a team.

9

"One. Two. One. Two. Keep in time," Nikki counted out loud as she and Carrie skated backward crossovers in preparation for the pairs spin. She had decided to give up on Tori's approach and use Kathy's. These were the same words Kathy had used when she taught Nikki and Alex to skate as a team for the very first time.

"Now step forward," Nikki said in rhythm with their skating as they moved into the actual spin.

But as she spun Nikki noticed that Carrie couldn't center her spin. She was traveling so far when she twirled that she was practically on the other side of the rink.

"Well?" Carrie called when she had finished.

"That was fine. I mean . . . I mean . . ." Nikki searched her mind for another word, any other word.

But Carrie was already laughing, and Nikki started laughing, too.

"I think the word you're looking for is *bad*," Gabriella called out to them from where she and Haley were practicing on the ice.

"Very funny!" Carrie called back.

"If you were any farther away, you wouldn't have been in the rink!" Haley exclaimed.

Suddenly Nikki had a great idea.

"Okay, wise guys. Let's see *you* do it," she challenged. She knew Haley couldn't turn down any excuse to show off.

"Why not?" Haley said, her eyes lighting up. "We'll be happy to demonstrate."

Nikki huddled with Carrie. "Now watch, listen, and study," she told her.

Haley and Gabriella took to the ice. As they began skating in preparation for the side-by-side spin, Nikki began a running commentary.

"Watch their positions. See how Gaby's weight is centered. You were fine there."

"Fine?" said Carrie, nudging Nikki lightly in the ribs. Nikki chuckled.

"You were in the right position," she said. "But your leg could have been lifted higher."

Gabriella and Haley each lifted their legs very high.

"Oh, I see—they're extending the free leg a lot!" Carrie exclaimed.

Nikki was impressed. "Yes. That's one place where

you went wrong," she said. She glanced sideways to see if Carrie was crumpling from the word *wrong*. But Carrie's attention was completely focused on the pairs skating. Her eyes were wide with excitement.

"See how sure they are on their blades?" Nikki asked. She hesitated. "I've noticed you sometimes rock on your blades. That's not good."

Carrie nodded. She didn't seem at all upset.

The second Gabriella and Haley finished their spins, Carrie turned to Nikki.

"Let's do it!" she practically yelled.

Nikki found Carrie's enthusiasm contagious. And watching Haley had made her feel competitive. Very competitive.

"Let's do it!" Nikki agreed.

This time Carrie's timing was much better. And her approach to the spin was perfect. But then she tried too hard to correct her rocking on her blades. As Nikki went into her own spin she could tell that something was very wrong. On the second rotation Nikki and Carrie collided and fell over.

Nikki sprang up and went to Carrie. The old feeling of panic came flooding back to her.

"Are you okay?" Nikki asked.

Carrie nodded and sighed. "Clumsy. But not hurt," she said.

She stood up and brushed the ice off her down parka and skating skirt.

Nikki studied her for a minute. "Carrie, can I ask you a personal question?"

Carrie shrugged. "I don't know what the question is yet," she said.

"Why do you wear that ski parka when you skate?" The parka was so bulky that Nikki was sure it was throwing Carrie's balance off.

Carrie looked down at the puffy jacket and mumbled a reply.

"What?" Nikki said, leaning in closer. "I'm sorry, but I didn't hear you."

"My mother makes me," Carrie said. "So I won't catch cold."

"Well . . ." Nikki was almost afraid to continue. She wanted to tell Carrie to take off the parka. But what if Carrie caught cold easily? What if she got sick from not wearing the parka? Suddenly Nikki remembered what her mother had told her. You had to let kids take risks sometimes.

"I bet your mom just wants you to be warm, right?" Nikki asked.

"That's what she says," Carrie responded.

"Wait here!" Nikki ordered.

She raced across the ice and off the rink. She knew half of Silver Blades was watching as she entered the locker room. No one was supposed to leave the ice during practice. But she couldn't help it.

A moment later Nikki sailed out of the locker room and back onto the ice. She motioned to Carrie, who was practicing her spin again, to follow her to the side of the rink.

"Take off your parka," Nikki ordered.

Carrie looked curiously at the stack of clothes in Nikki's arms. She unzipped her ski parka and slid out of it. Underneath she wore a thick multicolored sweater. Nikki could see a turtleneck peeking out at the neck of the sweater.

"Take the sweater off, too," she said.

Carrie's eyes widened. But she took the sweater off. Nikki handed her a thin green thermal shirt.

Carrie put it on over her turtleneck.

"The trick is to layer," Nikki said. This time she held out a very thin green and blue cotton sweater.

Carrie pulled the sweater on over her head.

"Now put this back on." Nikki handed Carrie her own sweater.

Carrie pulled the fourth layer on and smiled. "I'm warm," she said.

"Let's try that spin again!" Nikki cried.

The thinner layers didn't make the spin perfect, but Carrie's balance was better. By Friday morning's practice, the pairs spin was a hundred percent improved. And they had almost mastered a basic side-by-side pairs jump. Nikki was amazed at how fast Carrie was learning. She could already perform most of the moves in their routine, and her ability to skate pairs was getting better every day.

Nikki glanced at the clock. Only fifteen minutes left until practice was over. And it was the end of the week. On Saturdays, the Silver Blades skaters practiced their own routines.

"We should have another run-through," Nikki said.

But Carrie wasn't paying any attention to Nikki. Her eyes were riveted on Martina and Lily, who were way at the other end of the rink. Nikki turned her gaze in the same direction to see what Carrie found so fascinating.

Lily skated alongside Martina in a gentle, even glide. They moved forward on the ice in perfect unison. Nikki was surprised at the ease with which they seemed to skate together, especially since Lily seemed so bulky and awkward to her.

"They can do it!" Carrie said.

"They can do what?" Nikki asked.

Carrie didn't respond. But Nikki got an answer soon enough. With less flourish, but with well-timed simplicity, Martina and Lily performed a waltz jump–loop jump combination.

"They *can* do it!" Nikki gasped.

"And we can't," Carrie said sadly.

"Do you want to try it?" Nikki asked.

"Do you?" asked Carrie, turning to look at Nikki.

They moved as far from the other skaters as they could. First Nikki talked Carrie through the motions slowly. It was important that Carrie be able to do all the motions on her own before they skated as a team. They would be skating very close together, and more than one pair of skaters had collided in midair attempting this move.

The other skaters started leaving the ice. Nikki looked once again at the clock. Practice was officially over. It was time for school.

"Can you stay five more minutes?" she asked Carrie.

"Are we trying the jump combination?" Carrie asked eagerly.

Nikki nodded. She wasn't sure if it was too soon, but Carrie could do the waltz jump perfectly, and her loop jump was pretty good. They didn't have much time before the competition to get it right.

When the ice was empty, Nikki and Carrie skated to the center of the rink, where they positioned themselves ten inches apart. They skated side by side, slowly and then faster and faster, until Nikki called out that it was time for the first move—the waltz jump. Both skaters took off from their left feet, did half a revolution in the air, arms and legs open, and landed at the same time. But as they began the loop jump Nikki knew something was wrong. They were too close at the takeoff. And there wasn't time to stop. They collided and fell.

"Whoa!" Carrie said as she sat up, brushing ice off herself. "That was some spill."

"Are you all right?" Nikki asked.

Carrie nodded. "Are you?"

"Fine. I just feel stupid."

"What happened?" Carrie asked her.

"I'll tell you what happened," a voice from the sidelines called. "You smashed into each other and fell." Haley leaned over the railing of the ice rink, grinning. Gabriella stood next to her.

Nikki groaned. The competition had seen them mess up.

"You guys still alive?" Haley teased.

"Yeah. We're still breathing and kicking," Nikki answered.

Haley looked at Gabriella. "Guess that means yes. We can laugh now," she said playfully.

"Very funny!" Nikki called.

"Why don't you give up? You'll never beat us!" Haley called back.

"Is that a challenge?" Nikki got to her feet, offering a hand to Carrie.

"It sure is!" Haley cried with glee. "You aren't nearly as good as we are."

Nikki knew that Haley was just having fun. But every competitive bone in her body wanted to prove Haley wrong. Nikki knew she was a better skater than Haley. And while Gabriella might be further along at the moment, Carrie had the potential to be better than her. They would just have to work harder.

10

"**R**eady?" Nikki called from behind the curtain.

"Ready!" Jill called back.

Nikki stepped out of the dressing room and spun gracefully around, showing off the tight red leather pants she had just tried on. It was Saturday, and some of the Silver Blades skaters were treating themselves to an afternoon at the mall.

"What do you think?" she asked.

"Wow!" Tori exclaimed.

"That good, huh?" Nikki grinned and turned to look at herself in the full-length mirror.

"They look great, Nikki, but I was talking about the price," Tori explained, putting down the leather pants she herself was looking at.

"Oh, yeah?" Nikki twisted around, trying to see the

price tag hanging from the back of the pants. "How much are they?"

Haley and Jill peered at the price tag.

"Wow!" Jill echoed Tori.

"Two hundred dollars!" Haley cried.

"What?" Nikki cried. "Oh, no!"

She took one last glance at herself in the mirror and sighed.

"They do look great, Nikki," Jill said.

"Let's go to Larabee's," Tori suggested. "They might have leather pants just like these for much less."

"No time." Nikki glanced at her watch. "We have to meet Danielle at Super Sundaes in ten minutes." She slipped back into the dressing room to change.

"I can't believe Danielle is interviewing us for the paper about coaching Special Olympics skaters," Tori said.

"Do you think she misses skating?" Haley asked.

"I don't know." Tori shrugged. "You can ask her."

"I don't think she does." Nikki came out of the dressing room and returned the red pants to their rack. "It was just time for her to stop skating competitively. She needed a change. She really loves reporting."

"You're the quick-change specialist," said Haley. "Getting in and out of those pants so fast."

"You better believe it," Nikki said. She shuddered. "Two hundred dollars. Yikes!"

"Why did you want them, anyway?" Tori asked.

Nikki hesitated. "I don't know. I just wanted something special, I guess."

Nikki didn't want to admit the truth. She knew Danielle was only going to ask them questions about coaching for Special Olympics. But Nikki really wanted to impress Danielle. Somehow she had the vague idea that if she looked really good for the interview, Danielle would favor her and Carrie. Write about them more, maybe. And then, somehow, the judges at the competition would read the article and be impressed with how hard Carrie was working. Maybe that would help them win the competition.

⌒ ⌒

"Two hundred dollars?" Danielle exclaimed when they met her at Super Sundaes. They were all sitting in their favorite booth. "Are you crazy?"

"Nikki tried them on at La Chic Boutique," Jill explained. "That's how much they cost."

"Well I got some leather pants at Larabee's and they only cost thirty-eight dollars," Danielle said. "They're fake!"

"Enough talk about leather pants," Haley said, looking over the menu. "What are we eating? I'm famished!"

"Food later," Danielle said, suddenly very no-nonsense. She opened her knapsack and pulled out a reporter's notebook and a pen.

"No way!" Haley complained.

"Why don't we order first, and then start the interview?" Nikki suggested. "That way we can continue talking while we eat."

Everyone agreed that this was a great idea. They ordered quickly, and Danielle began by asking Jill and Tori about singles coaching. Nikki found her mind wandering. She kept wondering why she was so good at fixing organizational problems and so bad at fixing the waltz jump–loop jump combination that she and Carrie had been working on all morning. They had rehearsed it over and over again, for hours, but they just couldn't get the loop jump right. Nikki knew that they could do it. *If* they didn't kill each other first, she thought, smiling to herself. Her hand rubbed her knee gingerly. It was still sore from the final collision of the morning. She hoped that Carrie's arm didn't hurt too much.

Kathy had been wonderful. Nikki had explained that she and Carrie needed extra practice time, and Kathy had said they could use the Saturday practice time reserved for Silver Blades. Even Alex had been great about giving up their time. He was really enjoying working with Owen, even if he was "the only kid on the ice who's a worse skater than Stacey."

Nikki snapped out of her reverie when a steaming bowl of vegetable soup was placed in front of her. As she blew on the soup to cool it, she heard Haley say: "And now that we've perfected the waltz jump–loop jump combo, we're starting to work on the loop jump– loop jump combination."

Nikki almost spit out the spoonful of soup she had put in her mouth.

"That's an optional move!" she sputtered.

"So?" Haley said.

"So why are you doing it? This isn't the Olympics," Nikki cried. "Give me a break!"

Danielle leaned toward Nikki, pen poised above paper.

"Why are you so upset about this?" she asked.

"I'm not upset," said Nikki, surprised to discover how upset she really was.

"I think you are," said Danielle.

"And I think you're a reporter, not a psychologist!" Nikki snapped.

Danielle's eyes grew wide, and she backed off. Nikki took a deep breath and steadied herself.

"I'm sorry, Dani," she said, gently touching her friend's shoulder. "I didn't mean to bite your head off."

"That's okay," Danielle said, brightening. A gleam replaced the hurt in her eyes. "But now you have to answer the question."

Nikki laughed. "Okay, okay. What was the question again?"

This time everyone at the table laughed.

Haley answered for Danielle. "The question is, why are you so upset that Gabriella is a better skater than Carrie?" A mischievous smile tugged at the corners of her mouth.

"She is not!" Nikki said defensively.

"Yes, she is," Haley answered.

"No, she isn't," Nikki insisted.

"Then how come Gabriella can do the waltz jump–loop jump combination *and* the loop jump–loop jump combination, and Carrie can't?" Haley asked.

"It's my fault," Nikki said quickly. "I bet if we had started practicing when you and Gabriella did, Carrie would already be able to do both of those moves."

"No way, Nik!" Haley exclaimed. "I saw you two this morning. You could practice for years and never get it right. You aren't even going to beat Martina and Lily."

"*Ooh!*" Jill and Tori cried at the same time.

"Your turn, Nik," Danielle said.

"T-This isn't funny," Nikki sputtered.

"Sure it is," Haley shot back.

Nikki's eyes flashed with annoyance. "Since when do you take competitions so lightly?"

"Since I know I'm going to win!" Haley said smugly.

Now Haley was going too far. Nikki knew that her friend was trying to be playful. But to Nikki it really wasn't a laughing matter. She was used to winning. And she didn't like being challenged or laughed at.

"Carrie and I are going to win," she said, a little too intensely. "I have a whole program worked out. We have special practice sessions and an exercise program and tapes. I'm even looking into getting special outfits and skates for us! We are going to win! And we're going to look like winners!"

An uncomfortable silence settled over the table after Nikki's outburst.

Jill was the first to break the silence.

"Special outfits?" she asked quietly. "Don't you think that's a little too much?"

Nikki shrugged and turned all her attention to her soup. She was embarrassed about having yelled, and about the intensity of her little speech. Worse, she hadn't been telling the truth. There was no way she could afford special outfits or special skates. And, anyway, this was only a small local competition.

So if it's only a local competition, Nikki wondered as she lay in bed that night, why am I getting so crazy about it? She knew the answer almost at the same moment that she asked the question: because she had to prove that Haley was wrong. Carrie *did* have the potential to be a better skater than Gabriella. All she needed was a little hard work.

Nikki got out of bed and went to the phone. She quickly dialed Carrie's number. When Carrie answered, Nikki said, "Hi, it's me. Be at the rink at five sharp on Monday morning!"

11

Nikki knew that Carrie would have to wake up at three-thirty in the morning to make a five A.M. practice on Monday. But she also knew that Carrie would show up on time.

And she did.

They were the only ones on the ice. Actually, they were the only ones in the building, except for Bill, the janitor who opened the rink every day. He sat in the bleachers, sipping coffee from a plastic thermos cup, and watched them. Nikki didn't mind. She knew that when the day got started, Bill was usually too busy to sit down for any reason. If he chose to spend his few quiet minutes of the day watching two skaters smash into each other and fall, that was up to him.

In the stillness of the early morning, there were no distractions. And the skating surface was completely smooth. Nikki and Carrie managed to perform the waltz jump–loop jump combination without colliding, and without falling!

"All right!" Carrie cried.

Bill applauded from his seat in the bleachers. Carrie took a bow.

"Don't get excited yet," Nikki warned.

"Why not?" Carrie asked. "We did it!"

"All we did was not fall," Nikki pointed out. "Let's see if we can do it again. Only this time, make sure to shift your weight completely to your right foot before the loop jump."

They did it again. And again. And again. By the time the other skaters began to arrive at the rink, they could execute the move in a technically clean fashion. Nikki was thrilled. They had a long way to go in the grace and flair department, but with a lot of practice, they could do it!

At 5:35, Haley and Gabriella took to the ice. While Nikki and Carrie continued to practice the waltz jump–loop jump combination, the other two skaters perfected the loop jump–loop jump combination. Watching them, Nikki felt physically ill. There was no way she and Carrie could win without performing that move too. And Haley knew it. She kept looking over and waving every time she and Gabriella landed the move.

After practice Nikki took Carrie aside.

"You have to practice harder," she told her partner. "You have to be here at five every morning from now on. And I want you to practice the moves in front of a mirror at night. Okay?"

"Okay." Carrie's voice was a little shaky.

"Is there a problem?" Nikki asked.

Carrie shook her head. But her lips were pursed.

"Are you sure?" Nikki asked.

"No problem," Carrie insisted.

"Good. I'll see you tomorrow morning at five."

Nikki turned and skated back onto the ice. She hoped that she hadn't been too hard on Carrie. But the point of all this was to win.

By the time Carrie walked into the arena on Tuesday morning, Nikki was furious. She had been practicing on the ice for forty-five minutes. She'd spent the last fifteen minutes watching Haley and Gabriella. They were miles ahead of Nikki and Carrie, both technically and artistically. Watching them was giving Nikki a headache.

"You're late!" she snapped at Carrie.

"I know," Carrie said. "I'm sorry."

"Did you at least practice in front of a mirror last night?" Nikki asked.

"No," Carrie said honestly. She offered no additional explanation, which only made Nikki more irritable.

They moved into the section of the rink that was assigned to them for morning practice.

"Let's start from the beginning of the routine," Nikki said.

"I need to warm up," Carrie responded.

"If you warm up, we'll have no time for practice."

Even as she said it Nikki knew it was a mistake. Every skater, every athlete, needed to warm up to prevent injury.

Carrie knew this, too, and was firm. "A short warm-up," she insisted.

Carrie kept her warm-up very short, as promised. But the tension between them built. Carrie fell during their simplest spin.

Nikki sighed as she helped Carrie up. "You okay?" she asked wearily.

"Yeah," Carrie said.

"Let's just call it a day. We'll try again tomorrow," Nikki told her. "Try to be on time, please."

"I will," Carrie said.

"Oh, I almost forgot," Nikki said. "Before you leave the rink, I have a videotape to lend you. Watch it tonight. It will help you with your loop jump."

"Really?" Carrie replied. "Thanks."

"I didn't watch the tape, so go ahead and yell," Carrie said in her good-natured way on Wednesday morning.

"Well, at least you're on time." Nikki tried to hide her annoyance. Didn't Carrie understand how important it was to beat Haley and Gabriella? At the rate they were going, they wouldn't even beat Martina and Lily.

"I'll watch the tape tonight," Carrie promised. She bent over and stretched out her back.

"Do you want to warm up?" Nikki asked.

"I did already," Carrie answered. "I was here before you today!" She said it so proudly that Nikki had to smile.

They went right to work on the waltz jump–loop jump combination. They worked on it all morning, until they had it just right. By the end of practice, even Nikki had to admit that they were up to competition standards. The combination was clean, and even graceful. Carrie was turning out to be a truly lovely skater.

There were five minutes left to the practice session.

"Let's run through the whole routine once, and call it a day," Nikki suggested.

Carrie agreed.

They performed the routine slowly, deliberately— and confidently. Much to Nikki's surprise, they made very few mistakes.

"We're good!" Carrie said when they were done. She gasped for breath. "Can you believe it?"

"We are good," Nikki agreed, a bit out of breath herself, but proud of what they'd accomplished. Then Nikki looked up and saw Gabriella, head high and smile wide, skating perfectly parallel to Haley. They executed a glorious loop jump–loop jump combination.

Instantly Nikki's sense of accomplishment vanished. She and Carrie weren't the best—yet.

"We're going to nail that combo," she told Carrie. "Just make sure you watch the tape!"

As Nikki dressed on Thursday morning she had to admit that her nerves were frazzled. The week had gone by too fast. It was all a blur. Practice with Carrie early in the morning, then school, then practice with Alex, plus the pressure of the upcoming competition . . . it was getting to be too much. She hadn't been sleeping well either. Bad dreams about the upcoming competition kept her tossing and turning. And Ben had been waking a lot in the middle of the night.

She was also a little annoyed at Carrie. It seemed as if every little advance was a triumph for her new partner. If Carrie didn't fall, she was thrilled. For Nikki it was different. Every small improvement meant she had to look immediately to the next challenge.

Well, at least they were now as good as Martina and Lily. And they had a whole week to learn the optional move that Haley and Gabriella were going to do. It all depended on Carrie and whether she had watched the videotape to pick up some pointers about the height on her loop jump. That was really the only obstacle to doing the loop jump–loop jump combination.

"Good morning," Carrie sang out as she skated onto the ice.

Nikki glanced at the clock. 5:15. And Carrie wasn't even warmed up yet.

Nikki cut right to the point. "You're late again!"

"Only fifteen minutes," Carrie said. "I'm sorry. We still have plenty of time."

Nikki ignored the apology. "Did you watch the tape?" she asked.

"No," Carrie whispered. "I didn't watch it. I'm sorry."

"What do you mean, you're sorry?" Nikki exploded. "I'm not interested in your excuses, Carrie. Are you serious about this or not? If not, then stop wasting my time!"

Carrie didn't say a word. But slowly her face began to crumple. Her eyes filled with tears. She turned and stumbled off the ice. As she raced into the locker room Nikki could hear her sobs echo through the empty building.

12

Nikki sighed and chipped at the ice with her toe pick. She felt awful. She had made Carrie cry. She knew it was a mistake to criticize someone like Carrie. Yet they never would have gotten this far if Nikki had kept saying everything was just fine. They would never have discovered how much potential Carrie had as a pairs skater. She sighed again. It seemed like a no-win situation.

There were only a few minutes left before the other skaters arrived. Nikki knew she should apologize. She wanted to follow Carrie into the locker room immediately, but she stalled, wiping ice off her tights. Anyway, she thought, Carrie probably needed a few minutes by herself. Nikki waited too long, however. By the time she entered the locker room, Carrie was gone.

As the arena filled with skaters Nikki felt as if they

were all watching her, staring at a big sign on her back that said I MADE CARRIE CRY. Now how could she apologize? She had no idea where Carrie was.

"Nikki!"

Nikki looked up from where she sat in the bleachers. Kathy was standing almost on top of her.

"My office. Now!" was all the coach said. She turned and walked off abruptly, her ponytail swinging behind her.

Nikki slipped on her skate guards and followed, aware all eyes were on her. She half expected to find Carrie waiting in the coach's office. But instead, Sally Holmes sat inside, looking as calm and perfect as always.

"Where's Carrie?" Nikki asked. "Is she okay?"

"She's fine," Ms. Holmes said. "People have been more unkind to her than you were."

"I didn't mean to make her cry," Nikki said.

Kathy took a seat behind her desk but did not speak. Nikki shifted uncomfortably under Ms. Holmes's direct gaze. For what seemed like a long time no one said anything. The clock on Kathy's desk ticked louder and louder as the silence got thicker and heavier.

After what seemed like an eternity, Ms. Holmes finally spoke. "Why do you think Carrie got so upset?" she asked.

Nikki shrugged.

"Please try to answer the question," Ms. Holmes urged.

Nikki knew the answer, or what she thought was the answer, but she was afraid to say it out loud.

"Feel free to be completely honest." Ms. Holmes must have been reading Nikki's mind. "Nothing you say will go beyond this room."

Nikki took a deep breath. "Okay, then," she said. "I think that retarded people get upset more easily."

Kathy and Ms. Holmes exchanged a look.

"I really didn't mean to make her cry!" Nikki continued quickly. "I swear I didn't!"

"We know that, Nikki," Ms. Holmes said gently.

"No, you don't!" Nikki said loudly. "I saw that look you two gave each other. You think I'm mean. You think I knew what I was doing."

"Did you?" Kathy asked.

"I told you!" cried Nikki, practically in tears herself now. "I didn't mean to make her cry."

"Okay, Nikki, calm down," Ms. Holmes said. "And please sit." She motioned at the only unoccupied chair in the room. Nikki slid into it gratefully.

"The reason we looked at each other," she explained, "is that you said Carrie cried because retarded people get upset more easily."

Nikki nodded. She believed it was true.

"I'm not saying that Carrie isn't a bit more sensitive than you might be. But you can't say that she's like that because she's a retarded person and all retarded people get upset easily," Ms. Holmes said. "Carrie is an individual. She is her own person. She is a thirteen-year-old girl with Down syndrome who loves to ice-skate, who loves to dance, who hates broccoli, who cries when someone yells at her when she is trying her best. That's all."

"She hates broccoli?" Nikki asked.

She noticed instantly that her humor was not appreciated.

"Sorry," Nikki continued. "I guess I'm not comfortable with this. I think you're saying that Carrie didn't cry because she's got Down syndrome, she cried because I was mean to her when she was doing her best. Is that right?"

"Bingo!" Ms. Holmes said.

"Can I apologize to her now?" Nikki asked.

"Carrie has gone home," Kathy answered.

"I hope she comes back," Nikki said quietly. And to herself she added, I hope I haven't ruined skating for her forever.

Nikki called Carrie's home all night long. Sometimes there was no answer. Other times Nikki left a message. But Carrie never returned Nikki's calls. Finally Nikki went to bed. It was getting late.

When Nikki's alarm went off the following morning, she lay in bed trying to decide what to do. Obviously Carrie wouldn't be at the ice rink and Alex would be practicing with Owen. Nikki smiled just thinking about the shout of joy that had come from Owen the other day. Finally he had skated a whole lap around the rink without holding on to the side. It was such a triumphant moment that everyone had stopped skating to clear the way. And then Stacey had yelled after him that the two of them should skate pairs together. Everyone on the ice had exploded into laughter and applause.

Thinking about the joy of that moment made Nikki feel worse than ever about Carrie. She had been so focused on winning that she hadn't noticed how much Carrie had accomplished. Not even for one second. And that had been wrong. Nikki had really blown it. She wished Carrie would talk to her so she could apologize and tell her how well she was doing.

Sighing, Nikki got out of bed and started to dress. She would go to the rink and work on her own skating. Maybe she could send a message to Carrie through Gabriella.

~ ~

"You're late!" Carrie announced, pointing at the clock.

"Carrie!" Nikki dropped her bag and ran to the bleachers. Carrie sat calmly sipping hot chocolate from a Styrofoam cup. Nikki noticed that Carrie was wearing a layered outfit. And it was covered with bits of ice. She had already been practicing.

"It's fifteen minutes before six o'clock," Carrie pointed out.

Nikki grinned. "I'm so glad you're here, Carrie. I called you all night long."

"I know," Carrie said.

"I'm really sorry about yesterday," Nikki admitted. "I had no right to yell at you like that."

"I'm sorry, too," Carrie said.

"Why?" Nikki was surprised.

"I shouldn't have run away," Carrie answered simply.

Nikki stared. Carrie seemed to solve her problems so easily. Nikki really admired her for that.

Meanwhile, Carrie's eyes were glued to the rink, where Haley and Gabriella were doing their loop jump–loop jump combination. Next to them Stacey staggered around the rink.

"Fine. Great," Tori called to her.

"May I sit down?" Nikki asked Carrie.

Carrie patted the seat next to her.

Nikki sat down and watched Tori and Stacey for a while.

"Fine. Great," Tori said encouragingly as Stacey attempted a jump, fell, and skidded halfway across the rink on her stomach.

"Now *she* should be wearing a heavy ski parka!" Carrie said.

Nikki laughed. They watched the other skaters in silence.

"I guess I just really wanted to win," Nikki finally told Carrie. "I shouldn't have had such high expectations."

For the first time since they had started talking, Carrie looked away from the ice and turned her attention to Nikki.

"I like that you think I'm good and that I can be better," she said.

"You do?" Nikki asked eagerly.

"But you don't ask the right questions." Carrie took a sip of chocolate and returned her gaze to Haley and Gabriella.

"What?" Nikki was taken aback.

Carrie didn't respond at first.

"What questions should I have asked?" Nikki urged.

" '*Why* are you late? *Why* didn't you watch the tape?' " Carrie said.

Nikki thought about what Carrie had just said. It was true. She hadn't asked why. *Why* hadn't seemed important. The truth was, for the whole past week, the only thing that had seemed important was winning.

"Why were you late?" Nikki asked.

"Flat tire," Carrie said.

Nikki gasped. "Really?" Something like that had never occurred to her.

"The next time my sister was sick," Carrie added.

"Is she okay?" Nikki asked.

Carrie looked at her and smiled. "Thank you. She's fine."

In front of them, Gabriella fell while attempting a basic loop jump, but neither Carrie or Nikki noticed.

"I didn't watch the tape because my two older brothers wouldn't let me," Carrie added. "They hogged the TV."

"No kidding?" Nikki shook her head. "I guess that never occurred to me."

"I know," Carrie said.

"I'm sorry I didn't ask," Nikki said sincerely. "It won't happen again."

Carrie turned to Nikki. "I do want to win," she said, grinning.

"Me too," said Nikki, grinning back.

"So maybe we can practice extra this weekend," Carrie suggested.

"Yeah. And I have another idea," Nikki said. She had been thinking about it as they were talking. "Why don't you sleep over at my house tonight? We can watch the tape together and then come to the rink early tomorrow."

"Really?" Carrie's eyes opened wide with surprise.

"Really," Nikki said.

"I'll have to ask my mom."

"Great! And you can meet Benjamin," Nikki said.

"Oh, your baby brother!" Carrie exclaimed. "How old did you say he was?"

"Five months," Nikki said.

"Is he rolling over yet?" Carrie asked.

"Well, no," Nikki admitted.

"Then I'll teach him how!" Carrie announced.

13

"**C**ome on, Benjamin. Roll over," Nikki urged her brother.

Benjamin smiled and gurgled at her. But he didn't roll over. He didn't move at all.

Nikki, Ben, and Carrie were all lying on their stomachs on the carpeted floor of the Simons' family room.

"Like this, Ben." Carrie rolled from her stomach to her back. "Now you do it."

Benjamin arched his back and lifted his arms and legs. Then he laid his head back on the floor and stuck his thumb in his mouth.

"He's so cute," Carrie commented.

"Yeah. I used to think there was something wrong with him," Nikki confessed. The instant the words were out of her mouth, she was sorry she had said anything.

Carrie pulled herself up to a sitting position and

peered intently at Nikki. "I understand," Carrie said, then added, "None of my brothers or sisters are retarded."

Nikki still remained silent. There were so many questions she wanted to ask Carrie. But . . .

"What do you want to know?" Carrie asked her instead.

Nikki smiled. "How'd you know I wanted to know something?" she asked.

Carrie shrugged.

"Okay." Nikki pulled at a strand of her hair. Then she studied the rug so she wouldn't have to look Carrie in the face. "What's it like?" she finally said.

"What do you mean?" Carrie asked.

"I mean," said Nikki, taking a deep breath, "do you ever wish you didn't have Down syndrome?"

Carrie didn't answer right away, and Nikki was afraid she had gone too far. But when she looked up, ready to apologize, she saw that Carrie wasn't offended. She was giving the question careful consideration.

"Yes, I do wish that," Carrie finally said. "But not for the reason you think." She reached out and stroked Benjamin's hair. "It's not being a person with Down syndrome that's bad," she explained. "It's how everyone else treats a person with Down syndrome that's bad."

Nikki nodded thoughtfully. She really understood.

"There you are!" Mrs. Simon said in a cheerful but tired voice as she came into the room. She bent down and scooped her baby boy off the floor.

Nikki and Carrie groaned. "Don't take him away, Mom," Nikki pleaded. "We're teaching him to roll over."

"Sorry, girls—it's Benjamin's bedtime," Mrs. Simon told them. "Besides, he can already roll over."

"He can?" both girls cried at once.

"Sure," Mrs. Simon said. "Although he's doing it backward. It *is* kind of odd. Most babies do front to back first. He's a whiz at back to front. And he can't do it the other way at all."

Mrs. Simon left the room. Nikki and Carrie took one look at each other and burst out laughing. Then Carrie lay down on the floor again and tried rolling over both ways to see which way was harder. It looked like so much fun that Nikki joined her. In the end they decided that front to back was definitely easier. Clearly Benjamin was a genius.

"I think we should invent the ice roll," Nikki said.

"I think Stacey already has." Carrie grinned.

"Poor Stacey," Nikki said, and they launched into a new round of laughter. "Well," she added, "since we can't help Ben, let's go watch that tape—and help ourselves."

They headed down to the kitchen to make popcorn first. While the kernels were popping Nikki melted some butter and searched for salt. Carrie found two sodas in the fridge. They carried their snacks back into the family room. Nikki slipped the videotape into the VCR.

"I hope this helps," Nikki said. "I haven't seen this one yet."

When the snow cleared from the TV screen, the first image was a title: PERFECTING THE LOOP JUMP.

"Great!" Carrie cried.

Nikki smiled. She had never met anyone as excited about skating as Carrie was.

The tape lasted thirty minutes. Every minute was filled with loop jumps, preparations for loop jumps, what not to do during loop jumps, or how to land loop jumps.

Nikki and Carrie watched the tape three times. It was almost ten o'clock before they went to bed, which was late for a pair of ice-skaters who were used to waking up before the sun. They both knew they would dream about loop jumps.

In the morning, Mrs. Simon made the girls French toast and drove them to the Ice Arena.

When they finished warming up, Nikki and Carrie met at the center of the rink.

"So," Nikki said, grinning. "What should we work on today?"

Carrie giggled. "Anything but a loop jump."

Nikki laughed, but then said seriously, "I think we should do loop jump sequences. The tape said it will improve our timing."

They spent the entire time practicing their loop jump sequences over and over and over. By the end of the skating session, they were completely confident that they could now try to do side-by-side loop jump–loop jump combinations without crashing into each other or spinning out of control. But they were tired and achy, so they decided to wait until the following day to begin.

On Sunday they met at the rink in the afternoon. Nikki could tell that Carrie was a bit nervous. But then, so was she. It didn't make it easier that Haley and Gabriella were at the other end of the rink. Nikki wondered what they were practicing now—a death spiral, or some other really advanced move?

"Let's just ignore them," Nikki suggested.

Carrie nodded silently, and they went right to work.

They warmed up.

They practiced their spins.

They practiced their waltz jumps.

They practiced their loop jumps.

And then . . . they tried the loop jump–loop jump combination.

It was beautiful!

"I can't believe it!" Nikki cried.

"We did it!" Carrie threw her arms around Nikki.

"Let's put the whole thing together. Quick," Nikki said.

They calmed themselves down and started again.

They skated their whole program, with their combinations just where they belonged.

When they were finished, Nikki saw Haley staring at them in surprise. They had really improved. Nikki knew she couldn't get too confident yet, though. They were getting much better, but the competition was the following Saturday—less than a week away. Getting the moves down was only part of the challenge. They still needed to work on polish and grace, not to mention flair. Would they be ready? Did they really have a chance to win?

14

Warm-up time was over. The rink was empty. The Zamboni smoothed over the ice one final time—and then the competition began. Dramatically, the lights dimmed, and a hush fell over the audience. The arena was packed. Nikki took a deep breath to steady her nerves.

It was much too early to be this nervous. She and Carrie wouldn't be performing right away. First was the singles competition. Then the Unified Similar Pairs skaters would perform. But there were so many people watching this local competition! Nikki peered out from backstage and scanned the bleachers. She saw the families of Silver Blades skaters and the families of Special Olympics contenders. And thanks to Danielle's article in the *Grandview Gazette*, half of the high school had shown up. Nikki glanced over at Carrie to see if she was jittery. But Carrie was sitting calmly on the floor with Gabriella. They were stretching and chatting furiously.

As the singles competition got under way, Nikki pulled Carrie aside.

"Let's run through the routine on the floor back here," she suggested.

Carrie shook her head.

"Why not?" Nikki asked.

"We practiced hard all week," Carrie answered.

"So?" said Nikki.

"So we're ready," Carrie said. "We'll do what we can do."

"You are such a philosopher." Nikki grinned. "I admire you."

Carrie nodded. "Let me win," she said. "But if I cannot win, let me be brave in the attempt."

"I like that idea." Nikki felt her nerves relax a bit.

"It's the Special Olympics oath," Carrie explained.

"I like it," Nikki repeated. "Let's be brave, *and* let's win!"

"I like that, too," Carrie said, giggling.

The singles competition was almost over. Nikki felt her stomach begin to churn as the last skater took the ice.

It was Stacey.

She stood in the spotlight, her head held high and her eyes brilliant. She skated forward. She turned. She skated backward. She turned. She skated forward. An entire section of the audience burst into wild applause, standing up while they clapped and cheered. Nikki peered out to see who could possibly be this excited about Stacey's skating. It was the crowd of Special Olympics families, a group of about forty people. Much to her surprise, she also saw many others in the audience clapping and whistling. Somehow they understood that for Stacey the simple moves were a triumph. Stacey stood still, taking in the applause and grinning with pride. Then she skated off the ice and up to an excited Tori.

"How'd I do, Coach?" Stacey asked.

"Fine! Great!" Tori answered, hugging Stacey.

"Fine. Great," a voice whispered into Nikki's ear. It was Carrie.

"Ready?" Nikki asked her partner.

"Ready," Carrie said.

The pairs competition was about to begin.

The announcer called Martina and Lily to the ice. In the wings, Haley and Gabriella got ready. They were next. Then Nikki and Carrie would perform.

Martina and Lily skated well. Nikki had always found Martina to be a technically good skater, but lacking in grace and finesse. Lily, on the other hand, was a fluid, poetic skater. Her technical skills were also good. Watching her skate, Nikki couldn't believe that this gawky, bulky girl was so beautiful on the ice.

But as Nikki watched their program she found herself thinking that the differences in Martina and Lily's skating styles would work against them as a team. They skated in synch with each other, never missing a beat and never out of step. But their different styles did not complement each other. Next to Lily, Martina seemed to be working too hard. Skating with the same style was one of the things that made Nikki and Alex such a perfect pair. They seemed to feel the same emotions on each turn and each lift. They seemed to skate as one.

As Martina and Lily finished their routine Nikki smiled to herself. They had completed all the required moves, and had made no mistakes. But they had performed only the waltz jump–loop jump combination. Nikki and Carrie would also be skating the loop jump–loop jump combination that they had worked so hard on all week.

Haley and Gabriella were up next. Nikki held her breath. Here was the real competition. She prayed that Haley and Gabriella hadn't added any other moves to their routine—any fancy moves that she and Carrie couldn't perform.

But watching the pair on the ice, Nikki's competitive feelings gave way to true appreciation. Haley and Gabriella moved in perfect unison. Nikki didn't think she had ever seen two girls skate together so well. Of course, up till now she had seen only male-female pairs skating, but this team was impressive by any standards.

Haley and Gabriella rounded the rink with a series

of smooth crossovers and turns. Effortlessly, they began their waltz jump–loop jump combination. It was perfect!

Nikki held her breath. She watched their next move, a flawless loop jump–loop jump combination. It brought down the house. Nikki swallowed hard. It would be a tough act to follow. But she and Carrie had practiced long hours. They had watched tapes. They had breathed, eaten, and slept loop jumps. The two of them had become a very good team. They could do it. They could win.

"Nikki Simon and Carrie Swanson," the announcer boomed.

Nikki swept the image of Haley and Gabriella from her mind. She squeezed Carrie's hand for good luck. Then they glided onto the ice together. When they reached the center of the rink, they separated. Their music started, and Carrie waited for Nikki to give the signal to begin.

Nikki took a deep breath and positioned herself. Then she looked over to see if Carrie was ready. Her partner was in position and seemed calm and contained. Nikki gave Carrie a nod, and they began to skate their program. Nikki hoped that Carrie didn't get nervous in a performance. She had never thought to find out whether she would.

But halfway through the routine, Nikki realized that they were skating beautifully. Carrie's face was shining like the sun, and her skating was confident and strong.

If they could nail the loop jump–loop jump combination, they would win! Nikki could feel it in her bones.

Nikki set the pace for the preparation into the waltz jump–loop jump combination. Carrie glided easily alongside her. Crossover after crossover passed, and then they took off as one. Into the air, then floating, then half a revolution, and down. A perfect landing! And up again into a loop jump. The crowd burst into applause.

More turns, and more crossovers, and then it was time for the spins. It seemed so long ago that Carrie hadn't been able to perform even this simple move. Now it was almost effortless.

They performed on center, side by side, and got even more applause.

Before Nikki knew it, the crucial moment had arrived—the time for the loop jump–loop jump combination. Nikki emptied her mind of everything but the feel of the ice under her blades. She kept one eye on Carrie.

And they were off, and up, and sailing, and turning, and landing, and sailing, and turning again. The audience went wild. Nikki knew that they had done it.

And then Carrie fell!

The entire audience gasped.

Nikki froze. She couldn't move, couldn't help her partner, couldn't do anything. It was as if she were watching this happen to another team of skaters.

Carrie pulled herself up to a sitting position. Then

she stood up. A bit wobbly, but proud, she skated to Nikki's side. She took Nikki's hand in hers and raised both hands to the ceiling.

"Bow," Carrie whispered.

Nikki bowed.

"Sorry," Carrie said as they straightened up.

Nikki found her voice. "What happened?" she whispered.

"Ice rut," Carrie said. "I tripped."

They skated off the ice together. The other skaters crowded around them. Until Carrie had fallen, Nikki knew, they had been skating well enough to win first place. But now there was no chance of winning. They would have to settle for second. Nikki couldn't face anyone just then. She had to get away. She slipped on her skate guards and her jacket and raced outside.

15

"**N**ikki—wait!" Carrie ran after her.

"It just isn't fair!" Nikki fumed.

"Why isn't it fair?" Carrie asked simply.

"What do you mean, *why* isn't it fair?" Nikki exclaimed. "You tripped on an ice rut. If they had smoothed the ice down even once during the competition, we would have won!"

Carrie shrugged and smiled. "We came in second!"

"But we could have won!"

"Winning isn't everything," Carrie answered.

"Oh come on, Carrie!" Nikki cried. "Don't you understand? We almost won. We almost beat Haley and Gabriella—and everyone!"

"Don't *you* understand? We did it!" Carrie exclaimed happily.

"Did what?" Nikki stared at her in exasperation.

"The loop jump–loop jump combination," Carrie said proudly. "We did it. I did it. Perfectly."

Nikki said nothing. She knew Carrie was right. They had done it. But she didn't feel like celebrating. Haley and Gabriella had won. That was all it boiled down to. There could be only one winning pair. And it wasn't Carrie and Nikki!

"Are you coming back?" Carrie asked.

"What for?" Nikki was still deep in thought.

"To get our award."

Nikki didn't say anything. She knew that she should go back inside, where the awards ceremony was probably starting, but . . .

"I'm going to get my medal," Carrie said. "Then I'm going to the party."

"The party at the snack bar?" Nikki frowned. "It's a victory party, right?"

"Nikki, we *won*." Carrie frowned as well, as if she didn't understand. "We won second place. What's wrong with you?"

An awkward silence followed. Nikki thought about what Carrie had said.

"We were brave and we won second place," Carrie continued. "Lots of Olympic skaters don't even do that. And sometimes they trip on ruts in the ice, too, but they don't run away. You're being a bigger baby than Benjamin!"

Nikki had never heard Carrie sound so forceful. Suddenly Carrie's face turned bright red. "I'm sorry," she said. She started to walk away.

"Why are you sorry?" Nikki called after her.

Carrie spun around. "I got angry."

"So what?" Nikki grinned. "You made me listen. And you know what? You're right."

"I know," Carrie said.

"We did do it," Nikki agreed. "So second place is fine."

"Second place is great!" Carrie cried.

Nikki smiled. "Well, let's go get our award, then."

Arm in arm, they two girls walked back inside the Seneca Hills Ice Arena. They took their positions on the podium and received their awards. The audience cheered. Nikki and Carrie smiled and waved.

Watching the glow on Carrie's face, Nikki felt happy. She knew that Carrie was right. They had won something. She was glad that she had come inside to receive her award. But as Haley and Gabriella received the first-place medal, Nikki realized that for her the competition had nothing to do with Gabriella at all. It had nothing to do with Carrie, either. For Nikki it had to do with beating Haley. And the odd thing was, Nikki knew that if Haley and Gabriella had come in second, Haley wouldn't have cared. From the very beginning, Haley had understood Special Olympics in a way that Nikki hadn't.

At the party Nikki found Haley ladling punch out of a bowl.

"Congratulations," Nikki said.

"Thanks. You too," said Haley. She smiled as she

handed Nikki a glass of punch, and then she filled a glass for herself.

"That was a great loop jump–loop jump combo," Haley remarked. "Of course, it wasn't as good as ours."

"It would have been if Carrie hadn't tripped on the ice rut," Nikki said.

"Lighten up, Nik."

"Well, it's true," Nikki insisted.

Haley studied Nikki for a moment before speaking. "You know, Nikki," she finally said, "it isn't true. Gabriella is a better skater than Carrie is. That's a fact."

"No, it isn't," said Nikki.

"Sure it is," Haley said easily. "I know it. Gabriella knows it. Even Carrie knows it. You're the one who can't face it."

Suddenly Nikki knew Haley was right. Gabriella *was* a better ice-skater than Carrie. Carrie was a good skater, and a really hard worker. And Nikki and Carrie might have won if Carrie hadn't tripped on the ice rut. But all in all, nine-year-old Gabriella was a better skater than thirteen-year-old Carrie.

"If you don't believe me, ask Carrie," Haley said. "Here she comes."

Carrie and Gabriella appeared at Nikki's side. They were all smiles and giggles.

"Ask me what?" Carrie said.

"Who's a better skater, you or Gabriella?" Haley blurted out.

"Oh, Gaby, of course," Carrie said.

"Thanks," said Gabriella.

"But we still skated better than you today," Carrie told her friend.

"No way!" Gabriella squealed.

"Yes, we did." Carrie grinned at Nikki. "Right, Nikki? If not for that ice rut . . ."

"Right!" Nikki grinned back.

"We came to say good-bye," Carrie said. "Ms. Holmes is taking a bunch of us out for ice cream. She says we're all winners!"

"I think she's right," Nikki said as she hugged Carrie.

Carrie threw her arms around Nikki and hugged back.

"Thank you," Carrie whispered. "You taught me a lot."

"You're welcome," Nikki said. "Stay in touch."

"I will," Carrie promised.

Carrie turned, her eyes shining with happiness.

"Thank *you*," Nikki said.

A big smile on her face, Carrie ran to catch up with Gaby. Nikki watched her go. She fingered the second-place medal hanging around her neck and smiled. For the first time since all this had started, she really did feel like a winner.

that's sure to get her into *big* trouble. Could this be the end of Jill's skating career?

#5: The Perfect Pair

Nikki Simon and Alex Beekman are the perfect pair on the ice. But off the ice there's a big problem. Suddenly Alex is sending Nikki gifts and asking her out on dates. Nikki wants to be Alex's partner in pairs but not his girlfriend. Will she lose Alex when she tells him? Can Nikki's friends in Silver Blades find a way to save her friendship with Alex *and* her skating career?

#6: Skating Camp

Summer's here, and Jill Wong can't wait to join her best friends from Silver Blades at skating camp. It's going to be just like old times. But things have changed since Jill left Silver Blades to train at a famous ice academy. Tori and Danielle are spending all their time with another skater, Haley Arthur, and Nikki has a big secret that she won't share with anyone. Has Jill lost her best friends forever?

#7: The Ice Princess

Tori's favorite skating superstar, Elyse Taylor, is in town, and she's staying with Tori! When Elyse promises to teach Tori her famous spin, Tori's sure they'll become the best of friends. But Elyse isn't the sweet champion everyone thinks she is. And she's going to make problems for Tori!

#8: Rumors at the Rink

Haley can't believe it—Kathy Bart, her favorite coach in the whole world, is quitting Silver Blades! Haley's sure it's all her fault. Why didn't she listen when everyone told her to stop playing practical jokes on Kathy? With Kathy gone, Haley knows she'll never win the next big competition. She has to make Kathy change her mind—no matter what. But will Haley's secret plan work?

#9: Spring Break

Jill is home from the Ice Academy, and everyone is treating her like a star. And she loves it! It's like a dream come true—especially when she meets cute, fifteen-year-old Ryan McKensey. He's so fun and cool—and he happens to be her number-one fan! The only problem is that he doesn't understand what it takes to be a professional athlete. Jill doesn't want to ruin her chances with such a great guy. But will dating Ryan destroy her future as an Olympic skater?

#10: Center Ice

It's gold medal time for Tori—she just knows it! The next big competition is coming up, and Tori has a winning routine. Now all she needs is that fabulous skating dress her mother promised her! But Mrs. Carsen doesn't seem to be interested in Tori's skating anymore—not since she started dating a new man in town. When Mrs. Carsen tells Tori she's not going to the competition, Tori decides enough is enough. She has a plan that will change everything—forever!

#11: A Surprise Twist

Danielle's on top of the world! All her hard work at the rink has paid off. She's good. Very good. And Dani's new English teacher, Ms. Howard, says she has a real flair for writing—she might even be the best writer in her class. Trouble is, there's a big skating competition coming up—*and* a writing contest. Dani's stumped. Her friends and family are counting on her to skate her best. But Ms. Howard is counting on her to write a winning story. How can Dani choose between skating and her new passion?